Those Who Run in the Sky

Aviaq Johnston

Illustrations by

Toma Feizo Gas

INHABIT
MEDIA

Published by Inhabit Media Inc.
www.inhabitmedia.com

Inhabit Media Inc. (Iqaluit), P.O. Box 11125, Iqaluit, Nunavut, X0A 1H0
(Toronto), 191 Eglinton Avenue East, Toronto, Ontario, M4P 1K1

Design and layout copyright © 2017 Inhabit Media Inc.
Text copyright © 2017 by Aviaq Johnston
Illustrations by Toma Feizo Gas copyright © 2017 Inhabit Media Inc.

Editors: Neil Christopher and Kelly Ward
Art director: Danny Christopher

We acknowledge the support of the Canada Council for the Arts for our
publishing program.

This project was made possible in part by the Government of Canada.

Printed in Canada

Library and Archives Canada Cataloguing in Publication

Johnston, Aviaq, author
        Those who run in the sky / by Aviaq Johnston.

ISBN 978-1-77227-121-8 (softcover)

        I. Title.

PS8619.O4848T56 2017   jC813'.6   C2016-907725-X

For Marley. You deserve the world, but all I have to offer is this book.

And for Indigenous youth everywhere, you deserve a story where you can be the main character.

— A.J. —

Inuit have always journeyed through the months of darkness and cold, not with fear, but with skill and hope and wisdom.
    —*Proverb created by the staff of the Pirurvik Centre*

1

The Breathing Hole

The young hunter knew that the sky above danced in joy with northern lights. Since it was rare at this time of year, it meant that this day was going to go well, and that the spirits were on the side of the living, allowing them to carry on with their lives. He stood unmoving, hunched over a small, almost imperceptible mound on a large expanse of sea ice. Just off centre on the top of the mound was a tiny little hole, about the circumference of his index finger. Lying atop the little hole was a small Y-shaped piece of sinew from the heel of a caribou. The young hunter stared intently at the small piece of sinew, each strand of it as long as a sewing needle, patient and unblinking.

His hands were uncovered. He held a harpoon upright, ready to be thrown at any second, at any sign that there was life underneath that little mound of snow. There was hardly any wind in the air tonight, and the young hunter was thankful for that. He remained motionless.

For hours he stood in this position, hunched over the mound, alone.

And then it happened. The small strand of sinew blew away. The sound of the seal breathing sent a jolt of excitement through Piturniq, the young hunter. He stood in the dim twilight, holding his harpoon with careful strength and unwavering determination. Hours of waiting by the seal hole were about to pay off. He synchronized his breaths to match those of the seal. One ... two ... three ... deep breath and ...

Pitu threw the harpoon with all his strength, piercing the thin icy mound above the breathing hole. The harpoon struck its mark in the seal's skin, and Pitu

did not wait a second longer before he pulled on the rope that connected to the *sakku* and began to break the rest of the ice layer that covered the hole with his feet. He yelled to alert his partner, who was waiting with the dog team a little ways off. For a moment, the young boy and the seal struggled against each other in a fight for their lives, until finally Pitu was successful and he pulled the creature from its watery hole in the ice.

The seal growled at the young hunter, slightly winded from the fight. It tried to crawl back to the water, snapping at him while it went, but Pitu curled his hands into a fist and hit the seal on its skull, killing the animal instantly. He could hear his brother, Natsivaq, running toward him. Before putting his mitts on, Pitu grabbed a handful of snow from the ice and stuck it in his mouth to melt. Natsivaq was there a second later and whistled through his teeth. "*Uakallangaak*," Natsivaq said, a term that meant excitement.

Pitu made no sound or acknowledgement as he kneeled down, face to face with the seal. He opened the seal's mouth and transferred the melted snow water by spitting it out in a stream into the mouth of the seal. He did this to thank the seal for its choice to be caught, giving it water so that its spirit would not be thirsty in its next life. It had been a long time since there was a new catch. The ice had been particularly thick that winter, which had caused the seals to move on and seek a better location. Now that it was early spring and the ice was softening, the seals returned in abundance.

"All right," Natsivaq said, clapping his hands lightly in an excited manner. "What a joy, we will be eating seal meat!"

Pitu grinned at Natsivaq. Even though his hands were frozen, he left his mitts in the sleeves of his parka and took out his ivory hunting knife. It was customary for the hunter to do all the skinning alone when it was his first catch of the season. It was also customary for the hunter to have the first drink of the creature's blood, and Pitu was excited to taste it—he knew he would forget his frozen fingers and the blood would rush through to every corner and tip of his body.

He cut the seal open with expert efficiency, the knife seeming to guide his hands rather than him guiding the knife. In only a moment, the seal was open and ready for him to taste. In the distance, Natsivaq and Pitu could hear another hunter as a seal popped up at his hole, so the two brothers knew that they could at least have most of this seal to share among the hunters. When they returned to the village, the other seals harvested today would be shared among the families.

Pitu saw the steam wafting out of the seal's insides even in the bland light of the twilight that never went away at this time of year. He stuck his knife into an area of the seal's blubber, taking care not to place it in the snow, where it would freeze. Pitu pulled the sleeves of his parka to his elbows, making sure his mitts stayed in the sleeves as he did, and plunged his hands into the seal, feeling the glorious warmth as it began to heat the coldness of his body. Cupping his hands into a bowl, he brought out a handful of the blood and slurped at it.

It was delicious. Exhilarated by the taste, a burst of energy got him to pick up his knife again and cut a piece of meat to offer to his older brother. A yell in the distance indicated that yet another seal had been caught. This was Pitu's favourite of the hunting seasons. In early spring, the seals were coming in for calving pups. He wasn't surprised that this seal was a male, not bloated by pregnancy. After eons, the creatures had adapted to know when the Inuit on top of the ice were in a state of near starvation, so the males appeared first, and then the females followed a few weeks later to give birth to the new life that would feed the next generation of Inuit.

Three seals would be little, but enough. After having a few more bites, Pitu and Natsivaq gathered up their things and dragged the seal to a meeting point in the middle of all the other seal holes and Natsivaq yelled, his raspy voice screeching out, "Come and get some meat!"

Soon, the five other hunters arrived, pulling along the two other seals, which were both larger and heartier than Pitu's. Though he knew that he shouldn't be surprised or feel as if he was cheated, Pitu felt a pang of jealousy and wounded pride. He was the first to catch a seal that season, and to be the one who caught the smallest of them was a tease.

But as the others began to thank and congratulate him and offer their unending gratitude, Pitu's pride returned. It was he who was feeding the hunters, who in turn would feed the camp. He was the one who began the catch. Words of his father rang in his memory: *It is not about the size of the catch, nor whether you caught something or not. It is about what you have done, or tried to do, to help us survive another day.*

His jealousy was replaced by guilt. Often, if he were bested in any form, Pitu felt that jealousy quicken his blood. Then always, he was reminded of his ever compassionate and wise father. His father had died only two years ago. For a man so wise and kind to die before his time made Pitu feel small and worthless. How could he ever follow his father's greatness?

Ignoring his thoughts, Pitu began to listen as the men moved on from giving him their appreciation to other topics, such as marriage and his boyish ascent to manhood.

Tagaaq, the oldest of the hunters and leader of

the camp, spoke with a humorous nature. "Pitu, this seal is telling us you need a wife now." The hunters all grunted with agreement. "If you listen, it's saying, 'Find him a wife and get him married!'"

They all chorused with laughter, and in the bland light, Pitu felt his cheeks heat up as he blushed red. Bashfully, he said, "I only hear you guys telling me I'm amazing."

The men laughed again and continued to eat the seal until all that was left were the parts that needed to be prepared: the skin, the bones, and for later enjoyment, the intestines. Other various parts were put inside the sealskin, and they wove rope through holes they had cut to hold it closed like a bag. As they all began to wash their hands with the snow and get ready to drag the harvest and their hunting gear to their sleds, the dogs could be heard barking and howling in the distance, a clear sign of disturbance.

Tagaaq strode in front of the group, angling his good ear to the sounds. "*Nanuq*," Tagaaq said steadily. *Polar bear.*

Tagaaq could always tell what was bothering the dogs because he was the son of a shaman. His mother had been a shaman, a woman of spiritual reverence and fortitude. She had been a greatly respected leader, though she was blind and frail. Her powers passed on to her son, but he remained humble. In fact, he often denied that he was a shaman, saying that he only inherited a fraction of the power a true shaman had.

"Wait here," said Tagaaq, his tone still sounding slightly amused. He continued his stride ahead, only carrying a harpoon. He held it out in front of himself, taking deliberate steps toward the sounds of the dogs. A mighty growl rang out, closer than anyone thought it would be, then a great roar. In the dim light, suddenly Pitu could see the pale polar bear blending in with the white background of the ice and snow. On its four legs, the polar bear stared at Tagaaq, and Tagaaq stared back at the bear. Still, the tiny old man walked forward.

The two were face to face. The polar bear began to swipe at and circle the man. Tagaaq was just out of reach of the bear. In an attempt at intimidation, the bear stood on its hind legs, which ultimately led to its downfall. Tagaaq thrust his harpoon forward into the bear's throat and killed it instantly, and calmly. The bear fell to the ground and the hunters all rushed forward as Tagaaq yelled with excitement and the same exhilaration that Pitu was feeling.

"We will be eating polar bear meat tonight!" the hunters began to chant, excited to finally have caught enough to feed the village comfortably. The sky danced to their chants, the greenish, bluish, and purplish glow of the northern lights swinging and shining in sync with each joyful shout.

2

Feast

Pitu ran alongside the dogsled to veer the dogs left. Any minute now, the hunters would be able to see their little village. The sun had long since set as they gathered their gear and secured their catch. Now, the moon, shining in half-glory, replaced the twilight. Its dim brightness would still illuminate the village of *igluit* on the ice. As the dogs straightened their course, Pitu jumped back onto the *qamutiik*, his brother's sled made from frozen moss wrapped in sealskin as the runners, with planks of bones from various animals to hold it together and carry the tools and goods of the hunters. Soon, Pitu would be making his own sled to be pulled with a new litter of pups for his team.

The village was located on a large lake between rolling hills and small mountains. The ice was covered in sturdy snow, and it was thick enough to comfortably live there for several months of the winter. Of course, almost everywhere the ice was thick enough for that, the only exceptions being the floe edge—where the ocean goes unfrozen and the animals thrive—and the little inlets where the current was too strong for the ice to form thickly. There were fishing holes chipped into the ice intermittently throughout the camp, for when the harvest of mammals was tough and unforgiving. Pitu couldn't wait to see the looks on his family's faces, as well as the other villagers', when they showed up with a polar bear.

He got up from the qamutiik again to run alongside as the dogs started up a small hill. His brother did the same, to ease the load. It was not very difficult to keep a steady pace with the dogs. At the top of the hill, Pitu switched to the left side of the sled in order to direct the dogs in a diagonal path. Going straight downward would allow the sled to overrun them and drag the dogs behind. Pitu's brother stayed on the qamutiik, yelling out orders. "Oi!" he called, to instruct the dogs to run right.

Pitu enjoyed running with the team much more than sitting on the sled. It felt purposeful and energetic. Though directing the dogs with the whip and the precise shouts was integrally important, it made him feel lazy. He felt a constant need for motion, a responsibility to feel like he was doing the work.

It wasn't long before they made it to the bottom of the hill. Pitu jumped back onto the qamutiik, still feeling the energy coursing through his skin. He could run all the way back to the village if he wanted to. It would be foolhardy to do that, however. It's best to preserve energy for when it could count most. There was no way of telling what the future held. There was no way of knowing when the next time he would have to protect others around him would present itself. This is what Pitu's father had told him over and over again, time after time when Pitu would be the last child awake, the last one to stop playing. His rowdy behaviour had been troublesome to the old man. It meant a restless hunter.

Restless hunters meant long stretches of time without food. They would grow weary of the patience needed for hunting, the waiting at the hole for hours. Instead, restless hunters would wear themselves thin in search of an easy catch. Sometimes this resulted in the people under their care resorting to killing dogs and eating them. Restless hunters meant starvation, along with the terrible things people have to do to stay alive in those situations.

The dogs found the worn path to the camp with ease, making haste over the instinct that home was just another corner away. Ahead was Tagaaq's team pulling his hulking polar bear. They set a slow pace. Behind them, they could see and hear the other teams, two more groups, keeping up. Now that they were on the flatness of the ice, the dogs sped up, quickly surpassing the lead team.

As the dog team pulled him around the last curve of a hill to see his little village, Pitu felt an overwhelming sense of excitement. It was not only their first harvest of polar bear since the summer before last, it was also their first seal harvest since the beginning of winter. He wanted to share the joy that he would see on the faces of the families. Pitu was also excited to tell his mother that he'd been the first to catch a seal. He let out a hearty shout to alert those in the igluit of their arrival. His brother whooped with glee.

A crowd of onlookers gradually came out of their igluit to welcome the hunters back. There were an abundance of people: elders, mothers, young children, and men who were unwell or unfit for hunting. Children ran to meet the approaching group of hunters. They were jumping as they ran, their shouting letting all know that the hunt was a success.

The dogs began to slow as they neared the little camp. Tagaaq quickly closed in. The children, when they caught sight of the large polar bear, grunted out of incredulity and joy. They gasped and gaped. They ran back to their mothers, screaming, "NANUQ!"

The dogs stopped right at the edge of the village. Pitu's brother went to check the dogs, making sure that none of them were injured or thirsty, while Pitu began to unload their supplies and the seals they had carried for the rest of the group. Natsivaq fed chunks of seal meat to the dogs. Everyone in the village converged on the arriving hunting party, most of them going to look at the polar bear on Tagaaq's sled. Pitu saw his youngest brother reaching out his hand to touch the bear and quickly taking it back as if the touch had burned him.

"You don't even come to say hello to your

anaana? What kind of son are you?" said a familiar, amused voice.

Pitu turned to see his mother. There was a smile softening her wrinkles, showing her beautiful facial tattoos clearly. Her black hair, sporadically interspersed with grey, was braided, and her smile showed a couple of missing teeth from her age. She wore an *amauti* made of caribou skin, the fur thick and warm for the cold days of the season. He smiled back at her. "The kind that catches the first seal of spring!"

She beamed brighter. "*Alianait!*" his mother called joyfully as she came to hug him. "Oh, my hunter, you are growing too fast!"

"*Anaanaapiingai*. Hello, my beloved mother," he said, hugging her back tightly. He loved the little old lady more than anything. Pitu was adopted, so biologically she was his grandmother and Natsivaq was his biological father. That made no difference in their relationship as mother and son, though. He grew up aware of his real parents, calling Natsivaq's wife Puukuluk, an endearment for the one who carried him in her womb and birthed him. He also loved her with extreme ferocity. Natsivaq was always more than just Pitu's brother; he was his father and mentor. There was no real difference in their relationship, no dividing line between siblings or parent and child. They were both. Pitu had two sets of parents. It was a natural fact of his life.

Anaana went to Pitu's brother and hugged him, too. Natsivaq told her about Pitu feeding the hunters and how good of a hunter he was. Pitu listened intently, the words holding a resounding amount of assurance.

"He hunts like it's a part of him," Natsivaq said. "He stands perfectly still for hours. There is no labour about hunting for Piturniq. It's his natural state of being. It's like he can feel the animals in the ocean, and above." Pitu's insecurities quickly vanished as he listened further.

"Piturniq is truly gifted, Anaana," Natsivaq continued. "His breath is the breath of the wilderness." Anaana looked over to her son. Though she was smiling, there was something strange in her expression. Her brow was furrowed in worry. It made her look sad, despite her glowing smile. Her eyes were not hidden in her folded flesh, as they usually were when she was happy.

"My hunter," she cooed, her gentle, wordless admonishment making Pitu feel a confused need for reassurance.

Natsivaq also heard the soft reproach in her voice, the almost-sadness that she was exuding. They both ignored it, desperately grasping another topic.

"Did you see Tagaaq's polar bear?" Pitu asked. This prompt lightened Anaana's mood instantly. She raised her eyebrows joyfully. "Yes!" She spoke with a leisurely mirth, drawling out her words. "It looks delicious. I can't wait to eat some!"

Their comfort returned as they kept up a lighthearted conversation, treading over the momentary awkwardness. It was obvious that Anaana felt regret about how she had reacted to Natsivaq's praise of Pitu. She commented no further on the subject, instead saying that they should bring the meat to the iglu soon.

It was customary for a hunter's wife to be the one who shared and gave pieces of the game he had caught to others in the village. Pitu had no wife. There were still children to feed in his family, with his younger siblings from both sets of his parents, but Pitu took a piece of the seal—the ribs—to share with another family. It was all that he could spare of what was left. The rest of the seal was meant for his family. "I'm bringing these ribs to Amarualik," he told his mother.

There was a knowing twinkle in Anaana's eyes.

She knew exactly why Pitu was bringing the meat to Amarualik's family. The old hunter's eldest daughter, Saima, was his friend. However, people in the village thought that the two were more. "Give Saima a kiss for me," Anaana joked.

Pitu felt his face blush at the joke. He left the iglu, running from the laughter of his siblings.

Outside, the clustered igluit were dimly lit from within. Families were happy for the harvest. There was a group outside of Tagaaq's iglu, waiting to get pieces of polar bear meat to bring home to their families. Pitu reminded himself to go there to get some for his mother, too, after bringing the ribs to Saima. *Amarualik*, he scolded himself internally, *I'm bringing the ribs to her father, not to her.*

Pitu recognized Paninnguaq, Saima's mother, walking to her iglu carrying polar bear meat with both hands. He caught up to her and offered to carry the meat for her. She accepted, putting the hunks into his arms and washing little bits of blood off her hands with snow. "Where are you going, Piturniq?"

"To your iglu," he replied as he walked alongside her. "I wanted to bring you and your husband some ribs."

"Oh, how sweet." Paninnguaq saw the seal meat in his hands now, mingling with the polar bear. "You know how much Saima loves ribs."

"Yes," he said, feeling his cheeks redden again, "I remember."

"I heard you were first to catch a seal," she said while they walked quickly between the igluit. Once outside of hers, she grabbed the pieces of polar bear meat from his hands, one by one, and laid them in the snow. "I hope you know how sought after you are as a husband, young hunter. Many women would like someone as skilled as you. Now, go inside, give my husband those ribs."

Paninnguaq's eyes twinkled with the same interest that Anaana's had earlier. He was glad that they were outside in the cold, where the flush of his cheeks could be linked to the chill in the air, rather than the heat inside of him.

Pitu crawled into the iglu, clutching the ribs in his mitted hands. Inside was Amarualik, lying down leisurely with one of his younger children. Saima tended the *qulliq*, a stone lamp that used moss and seal fat to keep a flame glowing, warming the iglu. She was concentrating on the light, her face washed in the orange glow, as if there was no way darkness could touch any part of her and who she was. As he entered, she looked up, a vibrant smile replacing her frown.

"Piturniq, the Great Hunter," Amarualik said as he sat up, his young son hugging the man's arm tightly. He was a large man, full of strength. "To what do we owe the pleasure?"

"I wanted to share some meat from my catch." Pitu came forward and handed the man the ribs.

"You are a good man, Piturniq." Amarualik took the ribs one-handed. He looked them over, and gave them to Saima. "Very meaty."

Saima placed them on a rack near the qulliq, licking her fingers after doing so. She looked at him. "I'm going to eat it all. No sharing with the little ones."

"What about the big ones?" Pitu asked.

"They can eat the polar bear." Saima had a mischievous grin on her face. Pitu truly admired Saima's humour. She could bring a smile to anyone's face, cheer a child from a tantrum with ease. Her ability to make anyone happy was one reason that Pitu liked her so much.

As a friend.

"Piturniq, you must know that Saima loves ribs," Amarualik said, licking his own fingers, too. "You must know her well."

Pitu raised his eyebrows. Paninnguaq entered the iglu, taking Saima's place by the qulliq.

"I should go get some polar bear meat for my mother," Pitu said.

"Thank you very much, Piturniq," Amarualik said.

Pitu left, passing the polar bear meat that Paninnguaq had left in the outer section of the iglu. He stood outside for a moment, listening to the soft laughter inside. When he heard his name in their conversation, he began to walk away, feeling uncomfortable with the knowledge that they were talking about him.

Amarualik hadn't been able to go hunting with them today because he had badly hurt his leg on the last hunt when he slipped and fell into a crack in the ice. The other hunters were devoted to providing for the injured, and Pitu hoped that this reason would overshadow his true reason for sharing meat with Amarualik and his family.

There was no use denying it, though. He wanted to provide for Saima. He wanted to come home and share an iglu with her, to be her hunter and husband. Everyone else knew it. But he was shy. Too shy to proclaim a proposal.

"Piturniq!" Saima's familiar voice called from behind him. He turned to see her crawling out of the iglu.

"Saima," he replied.

"I have to find my brothers and sisters," Saima said as she caught up with him. "My parents want them to come home and eat."

"They're probably by Tagaaq's iglu," Pitu told her, "watching him cut up the polar bear."

"Yes," she said, her grin brightening his eyesight, "that's what I thought."

They walked the rest of the way in silence. It was not a long walk. The igluit were all relatively close together. The crowd around Tagaaq's iglu had lessened, but there were still a couple of people waiting for meat, children still playing with the discarded pieces. Before the two of them made it to the centre, Saima stopped Pitu. She went on her tiptoes and placed her mouth and nose on his cheek, breathing him in. "Thank you, Piturniq, for the ribs."

She gathered her little brothers and sisters and said goodbye, leaving him there with a dumb look on his face.

3

The First Dream

Pitu stood on the edge of a cliff at the top of a mountain, in an area he did not recognize. There was an ocean thrashing in turmoil beneath him, its rocky shore being smashed by waves, roughened by a wind he could not feel. A glacier rested in a valley behind him, holding stories of millennia waiting to be told to only those who could listen. He wondered how he had gotten there, to the top of a mountain beside a glacier, without encountering some sort of harm and with no recollection.

As far as his eye could see, there was nothing in the distance except for a little brown island, beams of sunshine illuminating it to look like a place of pure contentment.

Looking around, there were no signs of animals or humans. The only signs of life were the orange, green, and black lichen that covered large boulders that were interspersed throughout the mountain, the only splashes of colour against the brown-and-white landscape of rocks and snow.

Though he had no idea where he was, Pitu was not frightened. Nothing about this place felt threatening, not even the deathly cliff and jagged rocks at the bottom of the drop into the water.

Through the rubble of rocks, a figure darted around. It was the same colour as the boulders— brown and tan. It darted around some more, closing in on him, until Pitu found the precise moment it would be in reach. He bent his knees and extended his arms at the perfect time, caught the creature in midair, and recognized the narrow face of a fox.

He held it by the scruff of its neck. He didn't

think foxes would come this far up a lifeless mountain. There were no signs of nesting birds on the cliffside below, no signs of burrowing animals anywhere. If the fox had come up here, it was to see Pitu.

Pitu and the fox stared at each other for a brief moment.

Then, unfortunately, the fox decided to void its bladder, spraying Pitu's caribou parka in urine. He dropped the fox. It landed on its feet and stayed for a moment, staring up at him. Pitu paid no attention, preoccupied as he was with trying to wipe off the fox's pee from his parka. There was no snow around to help the process.

"Stupid fox!" he said with annoyance.

The fox, intelligently, took that as a cue to leave. It darted between the rocks and down the mountain. Pitu watched it go, the form swiftly disappearing from sight. Only a moment later, two or three breaths of time, the tiny little figure appeared at the bottom of the mountain, jumping onto the glacier, scurrying down a path that led to the ocean. Pitu's eyes followed the dot across the sheen of ice. It moved far too quickly to be real. In less than a minute, it was at the shoreline, where it jumped into the dark and angry water, and disappeared into the chaotic mess, as if it were a little snack for a child in the midst of a tantrum. With the fox's sudden disappearance, Pitu grew extraordinarily tired, stumbling and falling onto his butt to lie down. His eyes grew heavy with exhaustion.

When he opened them again, he was in the iglu, with his little brother Atiq's stinky feet in his face. Pitu sat up, the heat of the air inside keeping him warm as the blanket slid from his bare upper body. Anaana was awake, looking into the line of flames in the stone lamp.

Pitu had two younger siblings. Arnaapik was twelve years old, a young girl quickly growing into her role as a young woman. As a baby, she was adopted from a family that was passing through the camp as thanks for Anaana's generosity. They noticed Anaana had no young daughters to help her in duties at home when the boys were out hunting, and the family had plenty of children to take care of in any case. Arnaapik was already a skilled seamstress and knowledgeable of how to take care of children, having had to take care of her youngest sibling for years.

Atiq's story was more tragic. He was a young orphan whom Piturniq's parents had adopted when the little boy's mother died giving birth to him. Atiq's father had died only months before, and it was believed that this was why his mother had grown too weak to survive the birth. Since his parents did not give him a name, and his old grandmother could not think of a name for him, the people of the village began to call him Atiqanngituq, meaning "nameless."

Shortly after, Atiq's grandmother passed away due to old age. Pitu's family took the orphan in and decided to shorten Atiqanngituq to Atiq, meaning "name."

"*Anaanangai,*" Pitu said.

"My son," she said with affection. Her voice was thick, strained. He made his way toward her, manoeuvring around Atiq's splayed sleeping figure.

"What's wrong, Anaana?"

"I'm just thinking of your father," she sniffed. "Why are you awake?"

"I had a strange dream," he shivered. He'd never dreamt something so odd. "I don't understand it."

She nodded with a wisdom he could not understand. There was knowledge inside of her that Pitu would never have. Anaana changed the subject. "We're going to have to move camp soon, before the ice melts. We're having a warm spring and summer is almost upon us."

"I know." Pitu looked at his sleeping siblings.

Arnaapik sucked on her thumb in her slumber. Atiq was the only one who slept with his head at the other end of the bedding, often kicking Pitu in the chest or face. "Anaana? Are you okay?"

She ignored his question. "You know, my son," she said, her voice wistful, "you are ready to get married soon."

Pitu ignored this. "I think I will talk to Tagaaq about my dream in the morning."

"Yes, that is a good idea," she said. A yawn came and wracked her body. She smiled, looked at Pitu. "My dear son, I think we should get some sleep."

4

Visitors

Pitu's relationships had always been easily managed. He got along with anyone he came across, most definitely if that person were his family. He was an older brother that his younger siblings looked up to. In turn, he was a younger brother who admired his older siblings. Pitu was a devoted son and hunter for the village. There had never been any antagonism in his day-to-day life.

That is, until he came back from a hunting trip with the others and saw the new sled and dogs that sat solemnly in front of Tagaaq's iglu. Tagaaq hadn't joined in the hunt on this occasion, complaining of a bad feeling in his stomach.

Pitu also had a bad feeling when he saw the sled. His stomach churned uneasily, making him feel anxious.

He ignored the feeling, instead going to unpack the sled he shared with his brother. They were planning to move camp soon, and once they settled in at their summer camp, Natsivaq was going to help Pitu build his own qamutiik and raise a new dog team. He could not wait. Six puppies from the new litter were already set aside for him, just starting to learn to pull small sleds that children played with.

Saima's familiar laugh sounded somewhere behind him. Pitu straightened his back, turned in the direction of her voice, and saw her as she stood from the entrance of Tagaaq's iglu, waiting for another person—perhaps one of her siblings or another girl of the village—to emerge from the opening.

"Saima!" he shouted to her.

She looked over, her long black braids swaying with the movement. Saima called out, "Piturniq the

Great Hunter! What have you caught now?"

"Two seal pups," he replied proudly.

She said something to the person she was waiting for, then she ran straight toward him. Since the beginning of spring, all those in the village had begun to refer to Pitu as "the Great Hunter." He liked it, especially when it was Saima who said it, because of the way she looked when she spoke. Her voice was amused, joking, but her eyes showed a hint of admiration. Her cheeks blushed as she spoke the words.

"Oh, their coats are the whitest I've ever seen," she said as Pitu set the bodies of the two small seals on the snow next to the sled. "Will you share some with me?"

"Your father caught many more than I did, Saima." Pitu looked over toward the approaching convoy of sleds. Her father had healed from his injury and took his return to hunting like a man parched of thirst who found a reservoir of fresh water. He trampled across the ice, pounced on the dens where the seal pups stayed while their mothers swam in the ocean. Even at his advanced age, Amarualik was a force on the sea ice. The ride back had been tiring for him, though, since he'd done so much running from den to den. He and his son would break often and lengthily. Soon, Pitu and Natsivaq grew irritated by this, and told the rest that they would be heading back to camp at their own quick pace.

"I'm sure he did," Saima smiled warmly. Pitu looked away from her pretty face, not wanting her to see him flustered. Then, with amusement in her voice, she added, "But I would like some from your catch, Piturniq."

He looked back at her face, unsure of what to say.

They were joined a moment later by a man— no, a boy—that Pitu didn't recognize. He wore a caribou skin parka, but his pants were made from the fluffy skin of a polar bear. A pang of jealousy swam in Pitu's belly. He looked at the boy in curiosity. "Who are you?" he asked.

"I am Sikuliaq," he said. His voice was deep, powerful. Though he was smaller than Pitu, the boy made Pitu feel inferior.

"Sikuliaq and his father arrived shortly after you left early this morning," Saima explained. "They are on their way to Iglulik."

"Iglulik?"

"Our family and camp are there," Sikuliaq said. "My father and I have gone a far way, searching for my lost uncle who left in the middle of the night and never returned. Sadly, we found no trace of him."

Pitu nodded. Saima smiled at the boy. The jealousy flamed deeper inside of Pitu. He looked at her, and said, "I should bring the seal pups to my mother. I'm sure your father will be proud to feed his daughter tonight."

Saima frowned at his words. He turned his back on her and Sikuliaq, and picked up the two small seals, one in each hand. No sound followed him, and he left them there with no further niceties. His stomach flared with irrational anger, a feeling that did not come to him often. Whether it was at Sikuliaq or Saima, Pitu did not know, but his feelings were strong and he struggled not to run back to the two and push or hit Sikuliaq—or do something worse that would be too far to come back from. He'd lose his control and his aggression would be difficult to smother.

He put the seal pups into the small outer tunnel leading into his home and went inside. The space was empty; his mother had gone visiting someone and his younger siblings had gone somewhere to play. The qulliq was not lit, but there was still some warmth inside. Pitu sighed heavily.

Removing his parka, he went over to the beds at

one end of the iglu and lay down as the cold air began to spread through the iglu. There were far too many things roving through his mind for him to be around others. Hopefully when his family returned he would be clear-headed and would not mind the company.

The solitude did not last long. Atiq ran inside with an air of excitement. "Big brother, why haven't you come to join us at Tagaaq's?" He jumped onto the bedding, on top of Pitu. Atiq was a troublesome child. He was the youngest, and full of inexhaustible energy. Atiq was only still when he slept, but even then he was in near-constant movement, kicking and speaking in his slumber. The boy did not learn lessons easily.

"I don't want to," Pitu replied lazily. "I'm tired."

"Saima said she was coming to get you," Atiq said. "But you never came. Did you see her? Sikuliaq followed her. He's a hunter from Iglulik. Tagaaq kept talking about you. Sikuliaq wanted to meet you. They want you to come and meet them. The other one is Arnatsiaq; he's Sikuliaq's father. He's a giant!" Atiq laughed.

"You talk too much, little brother." Pitu closed his eyes.

"Come on." Atiq tugged on Pitu's arm, grasping his fingers and pulling them. "Everyone wants to see you."

"No."

"Natsivaq said you caught some seal pups," Atiq said. "Come on, Pitu. All the other hunters already went to Tagaaq's. You're the only one who didn't. It's rude to not greet the visitors."

"Atiq!" Pitu sat up and pushed the little boy away. "Stop! I'm not coming. I don't care if it's rude."

Atiq took the response in stride. He laughed. "How come you're so mad?"

"Go away!"

He snickered again. "I'm going to go get Anaana."

The little brother ran out of the iglu, leaving the sound of his laughter trailing behind. Pitu fell back onto the blankets, shutting his eyes tightly against his irritation. A moment later, another person entered the iglu. Pitu did not open his eyes, awaiting the lecture from his mother in silence and stillness. She remained quiet.

A weight sat down on the bed next to his feet. Pitu squinted his eyes open slightly, seeing that the visitor was not his mother. Natsivaq sat with his back toward Pitu, rubbing his face. He was a quiet man, only speaking when it was an appropriate time to talk. Pitu admired that about his brother. There were no lies clouded around him.

Natsivaq sighed, half-turned to look at Pitu. Their eyes connected. Pitu sat up again. He said, "I'm just tired."

"Oh, really?" Natsivaq spoke softly. "I saw you talking to Saima."

"I don't care for that," Pitu said. "She has a new friend now, *ai?*"

"Piturniq, everyone knows that you are in love with her." Natsivaq put his hand on Pitu's shoulder. "Even Saima knows it. And she is in love with you, too. Amarualik has been speaking to Anaana about a marriage, you know? So, Saima was being friendly to the visitor, but she likes you."

"I am not in love with her." Pitu nudged his brother away. The news about Anaana and Amarualik meeting about arranging a marriage was a surprise to Pitu. His stomach danced and his ears roared with the rush of his blood. "Why have the visitors come here?"

"They are tired," Natsivaq said. "They have been searching for weeks. Their supplies have been depleted and they are low in spirits. They needed company."

"So, they should go back to Iglulik."

"They think that Arnatsiaq's brother went out

somewhere to die. Arnatsiaq wanted to retrieve the body, but they found no trace." Natsivaq rubbed at his eyes. "Piturniq, they have heard many stories of you from the hunters. They are friends."

There was no more arguing. Pitu had to go and see the two from Iglulik. Reluctantly, he stood from the bed and put his parka back on, following Natsivaq from the iglu. They walked to Tagaaq's in silence. The dogs all slept like death. The children ran through the spaces between the igluit, holding in their laughter as they tried to hide from the one who was counting, soon to be searching for them. Mothers scolded the children, telling them to play in the hillside instead. It was a normal afternoon, but dread filled Pitu's gut. He was embarrassed for his outburst to Saima, ashamed of his jealousy toward Sikuliaq.

They entered the iglu, to find Tagaaq and a man sitting with Tagaaq's wife and Pitu's mother. The man was huge, a hulking figure full of strength. He had a large protruding belly, but he did not seem fat. The man smiled at Pitu, showing one blank hole where he was missing a tooth. "So, this is 'the Great Hunter'?" the man said. "Why, he is just a boy."

"Perhaps we should call him 'the boy hunter' instead," said Anaana.

"Piturniq is almost a man." Tagaaq laughed. "He is no boy."

"Come here," said the man. He patted an empty space between himself and Tagaaq. Pitu looked at his mother and saw a scowl on her face, no doubt angry at him for taking so long to come over. He went next to the old man and shook his beefy hand. No wonder Sikuliaq was such a stocky, bow-legged boy. The man asked, "Are you tired, boy?"

"Yes, very much," Pitu lied. "I did a lot of running on this last hunting trip."

"Ah, pup season is like that, ai," he said. "You must have had fun. Did you see my son Sikuliaq? He was going with a young lady to meet the hunters as they arrived."

"Yes, I met him." Pitu neglected to tell the man of his earlier rudeness.

"Piturniq is definitely our best hunter," Tagaaq praised. "Though he is young, the boy already possesses the endurance and discipline that men who have hunted their whole lives do not. Piturniq, how many pups did you catch today?"

"Two," he said, embarrassed.

Tagaaq nodded, like this information was not going against his appraisal. The old man's eyes glowed. "And how many did you catch yesterday?"

Sheepishly, Pitu answered, "Seven."

The visitor looked impressed. "Why did you catch so many yesterday, and so few today?"

Pitu shrugged. "It is better not to harvest too many pups at once, to leave some for the future. The other hunters also want to provide for their loved ones, too."

"You are a smart one," the man said. "A lot of boys your age do not think like this. They prefer to catch as many as they can … and then the next year there is starvation. Even I, at one time, contributed to a lengthy time without harvest when I was young. I'd caught far too many caribou for my own good. We had no room to bring all of them back to camp, so we were going to return for the last two, but wolves reached those first. The next winter was quite awful. I never once caught too much to carry again. I learned that the spirits do not let you find game when you have tried to take more than you need."

Pitu nodded. The wisdom in that story seemed quite obvious to him. Nature was a balance. The spirits let you have what you needed, no more. Only greedy people took more than they needed. Spirits do not like greedy people. He looked at his mother, seeing her worried expression. Anaana had been wearing that face for weeks now. He was beginning to worry, not knowing why she was always apprehensive and troubled.

Tagaaq's wife, Taina, spoke, her lovely little voice giving him words of extreme power. "Husband, I think you should start teaching Piturniq the Great Hunter to become our next leader. He is a strong and wise boy. His father would be quite proud of him."

"Yes," Tagaaq said, "I think so, too."

Anaana stood up, coughing into her sleeve lightly. "I am so proud of my little hunter. I must go and prepare some meat for the rest of my children. Thank you for having me. It was quite nice to meet you, Arnatsiaq." She looked at Pitu sorrowfully. "Goodbye, my son."

She left without another word, but the cold that her tone held reached into his bones and hurt him. He felt brittle.

Pitu and his mother had never had this awkward discord between them before. She refused to talk to him about anything of value when they were alone, and with others present she hardly spoke to him or about him anymore. Pitu wondered what he had done to cause this kind of distance from her. She had never once been angry at him, other than when he would misbehave as a child. Pitu and Anaana had always had a closer relationship than most sons and mothers, with a devotion to each other that grew with the tragic loss of his father.

The visitor began to tell Pitu about his missing brother.

Pitu could relate to taking a small amount of supplies and leaving in the middle of the night without telling anyone. He could understand the embrace of loneliness, the freedom it would bring if he went to live alone, to die in complete silence and solitude. He'd embarrassed himself in front of the girl he wanted, in front of a stranger, and now his mother's cold shoulder was pushing against him.

In that moment, that was all Pitu wanted: to go off into the wilderness, alone, without any tools, without any intention of harvesting anything.

5

The Elder

Arnatsiaq and Sikuliaq did not leave for many weeks as they regrouped from their long search for Arnatsiaq's lost brother. Pitu and Sikuliaq still did not like each other, but Arnatsiaq had started to praise Pitu as a great hunter as much as the rest of the village. The days grew longer as spring began to change into summer. By the third week, the village had packed their belongings onto their sleds and backs. Soon, they began their journey to their usual summer home.

The two visitors followed them for half of the journey. Saima remained friends with Sikuliaq, often ignoring Pitu since the day he snapped at her. He was too embarrassed to apologize for the way he had acted. Besides, he was also distracted by his mother's lack of affection and her constant worry. Tagaaq asked Pitu to visit him every day so that he could share his stories of wisdom. It almost happened without much thought. Taina had said he should become a leader, and suddenly, he was being taught how to be one.

They were camped for a night at the bottom of a small hill. Pitu was with Tagaaq when Arnatsiaq interrupted. "My son and I will leave for our home tomorrow," he said. "We would like to come and see you during the summer. Could we speak privately?"

Tagaaq nodded and dismissed Pitu. Pitu left them to their discussion. He figured Tagaaq would be giving Arnatsiaq directions to their late spring and summer camp.

As Pitu left the iglu, he caught a glimpse of polar bear pants entering a small iglu only a little ways away. He knew that this was the one Arnatsiaq and Sikuliaq had built. Not wanting to part on bad terms, Pitu made his way over and said, "Sikuliaq?"

"Piturniq?" Sikuliaq replied through the snow walls of the iglu.

"Can I speak to you?" Pitu asked.

"Come in."

The iglu was small, with only enough space for two men. There were caribou skins on the ground for bedding; since it was a temporary stay, there was no need for an area of raised snow to ensure comfort. Sikuliaq didn't say anything as Pitu sat across from him with his legs folded in front of him.

"I hear you and your father are leaving tomorrow," Pitu said.

"Yep."

"I am sorry for how I acted the day we met," Pitu said, rubbing his hair, trying to look for an excuse. "I was tired from hunting all day."

"You were jealous," Sikuliaq said matter-of-factly.

"Jealous?" Pitu asked.

"I know you like Saima," Sikuliaq answered, "I was told by all the hunters that you two are betrothed. And you like my pants."

In spite of his dislike for the boy, Pitu laughed. "They're nice pants."

Sikuliaq smiled begrudgingly. "I am betrothed to a girl in Iglulik, but she's still too young. Her name is Apita."

"How old are you? You seem too young, too."

"I am thirteen years old," Sikuliaq answered. "Once I caught my first polar bear my father said I needed a wife. He said my mother would be too busy to prepare all the skins and clothing now that my young brothers are almost old enough to join our hunts."

"Do you want to get married?"

"No." Sikuliaq looked down at his hands. "Not yet. I just like hunting."

Relief flooded Pitu's body. He was a good three years older than Sikuliaq, but he abruptly felt mature and ready. He felt like giving the boy advice. Perhaps all his lessons with Tagaaq were having an effect on him. He said, "If you do get married to Apita and you don't feel ready, just think of it as a partnership. You will live together, and she will help your mother with chores, and she will make your clothing, and you will provide her with food and warmth. I think it would be quite lovely, don't you? Someday, you both will feel ready to go further into your marriage, but there is no need to hurry."

Sikuliaq nodded. "Thank you, Piturniq. I think you are a good man. It's wise that the elders are teaching you to be a leader."

Pitu touched the boy's shoulder. "I wish you good luck on your journey back home. Hopefully we will see each other later in the summer."

"Yes," Sikuliaq said. "My father wants to return and find wives for the men in Iglulik. Right now all the women in our village are either too young or related too closely to the men."

With shock, Pitu said goodbye and left the iglu. Coming back for wives? That was preposterous. Most of the girls in Pitu's camp were also too young to be married, or were related to the men of the village. But he realized that, though there were people who were related to each other between the two villages, there were still families that were not closely connected. That was what Arnatsiaq was thinking of. What would that mean for Pitu and Saima? They were not cousins, but was that enough for Saima's parents to wait for Pitu if a man came from Iglulik and asked to marry her?

Energy surged within him. Pitu needed to find Saima and apologize to her for his behaviour. He saw three girls watching the children playing between rocks on the hillside. They were yelling at the children to come home to eat and sleep. He thought he could recognize Saima's voice.

Pitu ran over to them as the children began to

stop playing and went to their older sisters or aunties. He saw that neither of the girls coming toward him was Saima. One was his sister Arnaapik, and the other was his cousin Panipak. The knowing smiles plastered over their faces told him that it was Saima who was the last girl waiting for the rest of the children.

"Saima," Pitu said as he came up behind her.

She ignored him briefly, instead calling out to the boys still playing in the rocks. Pitu recognized his little brother Atiq among them.

"Saima," Pitu said again.

"What do you want, Great Hunter?" She spoke without turning around to look at him, her words biting.

"Saima, I'm sorry," he said. "I was wrong to treat you the way I did. I was jealous of that boy, and it made me angry. I will never do that to you again. I promise."

She turned her head, but not the rest of her body, to look at him. "You were jealous? Why? He's only a boy."

"He has caught a polar bear." Pitu shrugged. "And you smiled at him. For a moment, I thought you were looking at him the way you look at me."

Saima did not answer him for a moment. She turned her gaze back to the boys and yelled at them to go home. Her tone was firm. The remaining boys knew that they would not get away with ignoring her calls any longer. They listened and made their ways home. Atiq playfully hit Pitu in the arm as he ran away.

Finally, Saima looked at Pitu straight on. There was a resolute anger in her gaze. "How could you think I would look at another boy the way I look at you?"

"I don't know, Saima," he answered, touching her arm. "I can feel the seal underneath the ice or the birds in the skies. I understand the way the waves move in the summer, and the way the wind blows in the winter. Nature is where I know everything, but when I am with you, it changes. You make me forget how to act."

"It's not my fault that you can't understand how to be around people, Piturniq." Saima took a step back. "Perhaps you should ask Tagaaq to teach you of these things."

Though Pitu tried to keep talking to her, she'd said her piece, and she refused to speak more. They walked to their families' igluit in silence. She tried to leave him before he could say another word, but he took hold of her arm and whispered, "I promise that I will never treat you badly ever again."

"You think all I want is a promise?" She shook her head, pried his hand from her arm, and went into her iglu.

That night, Pitu dreamt of a fox standing on a block of ice floating in the calm waters of the ocean he had dreamt about previously. Pitu was in a *qajaq*, paddling behind the fox. The sun shone brightly, unlike last time when the sky had been an upset shade of grey, assisting the winds and oceans as they thrashed against the world. It seemed that the fox was controlling the direction of the current, for when it changed the way it faced, the ice block would follow.

The glacier in the valley of mountains was behind, still resting peacefully, melting in the sunlight. Ahead was a fjord, and in the middle of it was the same single island with the sun shining a strong ray of light on it. As Pitu trailed behind the fox, a storm brewed around him. He began to feel tired, his eyelids growing heavy.

I thought dreams were supposed to reflect your life, Pitu thought as he woke in the morning. His little siblings were sound asleep. Anaana was nowhere in sight, but the light of the qulliq was strong, so she must have left only a moment before. Pitu dressed in his clothes and woke his siblings, telling them to go outside and look at the horizon in order to have a long life (and pee) and then to start packing everything for their trip. He left the iglu to find Natsivaq and his puukuluk talking by the qamutiik.

Natsivaq looked up and saw Pitu approaching, but he waved him away and gestured toward Tagaaq's iglu.

Around him, the sleds were being packed, skins and furs piled atop and tied down with ropes, and bags secured, keeping the everyday tools of those families safe during the day's journey. The dogs had been well rested and fed the night before, and were being set up for another long day of hauling the families and their lives. Pitu reached Tagaaq's just as the elder was leaving his home. He looked up at Pitu. "Piturniq!" he said. "Right on time. I need you to come with me to the top of that hill."

Tagaaq pointed to a hill that could almost be called a mountain. Pitu said, "I think that hill is too steep to climb."

Tagaaq nodded. "I agree. Perhaps if we go from a ways back over in the direction we came in from. The little valley we passed through had more gradual inclines."

They took a smaller sled that Tagaaq used to carry supplies. The dogs pulled them swiftly to the valley in question. They dug an anchor made of caribou antler into the snow and began a slow climb to the top of the hill.

The climb, though not as steep as it could have been, was still laborious. The two stopped a couple of times to catch their breaths, but continued up. Once they reached the top, they uncovered a pile of rocks. Tagaaq pointed at them. "You will build an *inuksuk* to mark Arnatsiaq's way on his return to us in the summer. I will speak to the wind."

Before Tagaaq turned away, Piturniq asked,

"Is it true that Arnatsiaq will return for wives to bring back to Iglulik?"

Tagaaq tightened his lips into a thin line. "Yes," he said, "but he will be bringing other women also."

"Do you think it is unfair for the women?"

"Yes and no," the elder answered. "It is unfair for women to live without a suitable husband. Marriages are more than a husband and a wife; they are an important part of our survival. Men need women much more than they need us."

"That's what I told Sikuliaq," Pitu replied, nodding. "They are partnerships, a husband provides for his wife and she provides for him."

"Yes, Piturniq." Tagaaq grinned crookedly. "Fathers and mothers could grow tired of providing for a daughter that can marry, and this leads to neglect. They can also neglect a son who hunts, because there would be too much food in the one family, and this leads to waste."

That was enough for them. Without another word, they turned their backs on each other. Pitu began to build the inuksuk, strategically piling the rocks so that the winds could not topple them over. He didn't quite understand why Tagaaq was speaking to the wind. He also didn't know what that meant, but he chose not to question it. Though Tagaaq was not a shaman, he had a gift with nature better than the rest of those in their village had. This is why he was a good leader. He could read the air better than anyone, and he always knew when there were blizzards on their way.

Pitu thought of the first time he saw a shaman. Though the spiritual leaders were not uncommon, Anaana had never wanted Pitu exposed to their shows of revelry. Once, Pitu had gotten furious and pleaded with his father, asking to go with him to the large iglu they called a *qaggiq*. The qaggiq was made by building four regular-sized igluit that could each hold a whole family as the base, then connecting them together with blocks in between each iglu and building a roof on top. These igluit could hold all the people in the village, and people from other camps, as they all gathered in one central location to celebrate the return of the sun after the long and harsh months of cold darkness.

His father had laughed and said something to Anaana that Pitu did not quite understand. "He will need to see it at some point in his life."

That night, he was in the qaggiq, sitting on his father's lap. Anaana sat next to them. There were benches made of snow packed hard together going all the way round the iglu's interior, with a large open space in the centre. At the edges of the circle the people were all gathered, and a man stood solitarily in the middle. He held a drum with one drumstick in his hand and he wore a parka made from some of the most beautiful sealskin Pitu had ever seen. His face was covered with weather-beaten skin, and long, black hair as dark as a cloudy night sky fell from his head like a waterfall.

The man, whom Pitu knew to be the shaman called Imiqqutailaq, began a steady and low drumming. The drum was made from the skin of a caribou stretched over a piece of driftwood that was found on a beach. The drum was large and round, the wood having been softened into a circle shape. A handle protruded from it, wrapped in sealskin that matched the shaman's parka. He held it outward, hitting the wooden rim of the drum rather than the skin of its centre.

He sang, in a hoarse yet strong voice, a song of his own experiences. Though drumming was not practised solely by shamans, it was different to witness a shaman sing, drum, and dance. The songs were usually sung by the wives of the drummer as he danced while beating the drum, but Imiqqutailaq chose to sing his own songs. The energy from his movements and his voice reached throughout the iglu and touched each person, leaving them all with a sense of joy and

awe. Pitu stared at the man, unable to tear his eyes away. Imiqqutailaq's hair swayed as he danced in imitation of a polar bear, as he chanted and sang about traversing the spiritual world in an attempt to appease the spirits that withheld game. He continued to sing, telling the story of how his people had been starving to death and how he had to meet with the deities to ask why they were angry. Imiqqutailaq ended the song by reciting the work he did to make the spirits happy again, in order to set the animals free to be caught by the starving Inuit of his village.

When the shaman finished his drum dance, he pointedly stared at each of the onlookers. Without another word, he walked away from the middle of the qaggiq, and sat next to a young woman holding a small infant. Imiqqutailaq's song had been a harrowing journey, full of intense harshness, yet as he returned to his wife and child, the shaman smiled softly.

Pitu had been mesmerized by the incredible story, and by the quiet modesty of the shaman. Through all of Imiqqutailaq's trouble, he remained strong and peaceful. At the tender age of eight, Pitu vowed that he would never dwell on his troubles and he would strive to live a life worth those troubles. He would always address his problems, and deal with what would happen.

It was easier to make a promise than to keep it. Especially when that promise was made to yourself.

"Stop," Tagaaq said. Pitu shook his head from the daydream and turned to face the old man. Tagaaq looked at Pitu oddly, his head tilted slightly to the side. "My dear boy, what were you thinking of?"

Pitu stuck out his lower lip and shrugged. "What do you mean?"

"The winds went silent, as if a storm were suddenly upon us." Still, the old man looked at Pitu with a funny gaze. "They whispered of good things, sunny days, and safe journeys. Then a moment later, the winds silenced, danced around you for a moment, and left."

None of this made sense to Pitu. He wrinkled his nose and said, "I don't know what you speak of."

Tagaaq's eyes looked past Pitu and focused on the inuksuk. A small expression of astonishment appeared on his face. "That is a perfect inuksuk. I think we should leave now," he said.

The climb down the hill was much less strenuous and time consuming than the climb up had been. They took out the caribou antler anchor and urged the dogs back to camp. From their position only a small valley away, they could see that the people were already packed and ready to leave.

Just before they reached the camp, Tagaaq spoke lowly to Pitu. "Boy, we have to speak later today. Once we stop for the night, you must find me."

"Okay," Pitu replied, confused. The old man nodded. They went their separate ways, Tagaaq to his family and the gathered group of hunters, and Pitu to his mother. She smiled at him brightly, her eyes disappearing into the wrinkles on her face.

A surge of emotion made Pitu tremble. He hadn't seen his mother look at him like that in weeks. He smiled back at her and coughed away the feeling in his throat. Anaana jerked her head back softly, indicating that she would like him to come closer to her. He did as he was directed. Anaana, so little and frail, stood on the tips of her toes only to reach his shoulders. Pitu bent down, and she laid her nose onto his cheek and inhaled softly, showing the affection that had been absent for what felt like months.

They said nothing. Anaana went to gather the little children, grabbing a strong hold of Atiq. Pitu went to his older siblings and helped them finish packing and preparing the dogs. He gathered the puppies and urged his young sisters and cousins to allow a puppy, sometimes two, into their small amautiit. There was only one puppy left and no more little girls to give it to. Pitu picked up the little husky. It was a female with black-and-white markings.

Families were beginning to leave on their sleds. Pitu caught a glimpse of Saima saying goodbye to Arnatsiaq and Sikuliaq. He put the last puppy into the pouch pocket on the front of his parka, which he had specifically asked his mother to sew for him for the convenience he saw in it, and raced forward. He did not want to leave the men on bad terms. Saima was going back to her family, but Pitu wasn't going for her benefit. He knew he needed to give her space while he figured out a way to prove to her that he was sorry.

Arnatsiaq stuck out his hand for Pitu to shake. The man said, "I look forward to seeing you again in the summer. Perhaps you will be towing a beluga when we see each other again."

"Maybe." Pitu indulged in the praise.

He went over to Sikuliaq and said his goodbyes. The two seemed to have let go of any animosity between them. Before leaving, Sikuliaq said to Pitu, "Saima still likes you. She's just mad."

Pitu raised his eyebrows. *Yep.* He already knew that.

Abruptly, Arnatsiaq said, "She doesn't just want a husband, dear boy, she wants friendship. An apology won't fix her hurt feelings. You have to show her your devotion. My wife did this to me when we were children, too."

It was as if the father-son duo thought that stating the obvious was some form of help. Pitu thanked them and bid them farewell. He ran back to his family, cradling the puppy in his pocket, making sure to not rock her back and forth. He dropped the puppy into Anaana's lap. The women and children were already sitting on the sleds. Without hesitation, Pitu sprinted forward and got the dogs running. Natsivaq did the same. Soon, they were off.

The sun was low in the sky when they stopped for the night. By this time of the year, the sun only set for a few hours per night. In only a couple more weeks, the sun would be in the cloudless and warm blue sky at all hours of the day and night, without even grazing against the edge of the horizon. It was a joyous time of year, bringing much happiness to the people and not only bountiful animals, but lusciously juicy vegetation. It also brought things that were not as enjoyable: unpredictable weather conditions, thin ice, and slushy snow.

After setting up the tent for his mother and siblings on a patch of dry earth, Pitu left to find Tagaaq. The elder sat next to his sealskin tent with a piece of soapstone and a rough, sharp-edge rock that had been made into a tool for carving. He carved the soapstone into a small figurine of a man. The elder squinted up as Pitu approached. His mouth twisted into an awkward smile.

Unsure of how to proceed, Pitu simply sat down next to the old man. Tagaaq continued to manoeuvre his tool against the stone. The roundish, man-shaped stone grew more defined: first with a head and shoulders, then grooves along the sides of the upper half for his arms, and a groove in the centre of the bottom half for his legs. Tagaaq said nothing. Pitu waited.

It could have been ages before the old man finally stopped carving. A distinguished little hunter was in the palm of his now dusty hands. There were even dents in the man's face to show an expression of determination—a hard line for his mouth, round eyes with furrowed brows. Tagaaq packed his tool into a sealskin container next to him. Then he stood and told Pitu to follow him.

They didn't walk very far, just around a hill to be alone and out of earshot. They were at the edge of a large pool of water covered in bright blue ice. Tagaaq still held the stone man in his hand. He began to tell a story.

"My mother passed away long before you breathed on this earth," he began. Pitu snapped to attention. He'd heard stories of Tagaaq's mother before.

"She was very young when the camp leader at the time said she had the gift of shamans. My grandfather did not want her to be taught in the ways of shamans. He was frightened. This news came during a troubling time at the camp, you see. They had been starving on and off for weeks, living off little scraps of food and a small fish here and there, but never anything truly satisfying. At one point, they had to boil their own clothes to get nutrients from the skins they wore. The hunters always caught one seal in the nick of time, but many elders passed away that year due to starvation. They starved themselves so their grandchildren could eat. And many children became ill and died, too. They had grown too weak to carry on.

"My grandfather was afraid of my mother learning to be a shaman because the spirits frightened him. They were too tricky. It was apparent to him that this starvation was not for a lack of animals, but because the spirits were bored, and were playing games with them. He thought they were hiding the animals in fog, allowing one seal to be caught only when it was desperately needed to see how long the people would last. If my mother became a shaman, he imagined the spirits dragging her away for their appeasement.

"But the shaman who would train her spoke to my grandfather. His name was Qilak. Qilak told my grandfather that he had grown too weak to speak to the spirits clearly. They'd grown restless. This, of course, did not make my grandfather feel any better, but Qilak was a wise elder. The shaman told my grandfather, 'She is a strong one, and she has the will and power to vanquish the curse these spirits have thrust upon us.'"

Tagaaq smiled, his missing tooth allowing a whistle from his mouth. "My grandfather remained unconvinced, but he trusted the shaman. He allowed my mother to go to the old man's iglu, where he lived with his elderly wife. She learned very quickly because she wanted the starvation to end. Her baby brother had grown ill and she was desperate to find a way to make him better, too.

"One night, when her little brother's breathing was shallow and slow, my mother ran from the iglu and stole her father's dog team. She rode until her eyes froze shut, and the dogs tired themselves out and stopped. They fell asleep, and she walked blindly until she was in utter silence. She cried for an answer; her screams pierced the nothingness around her. Though her eyes were shut, she could feel the spirits gathering, their lights surrounding her. She cried for their forgiveness and their mercy."

The elder rubbed his eyes for a moment, but his tone of voice did not change. "When finally she stopped crying and she felt that the spirits no longer surrounded her, she rubbed her eyes to warm them up, but still she could not see. Unafraid, she whistled for the dogs to find her as she felt the ground for her old footprints. When she found the dogs and they ran back to their camp, she could hear the relief and the sadness from the people all around her. She was brought to her family's iglu only to find that her baby brother had passed away. She could not cry for her brother. Her eyes had gone dry and dead. Though she could see nothing, she strode forward without help, and she found her little brother's coldness and kissed his cheeks and forehead. Then she left the iglu, telling the hunters that a polar bear had followed her back to the village.

"Sure enough, her words were true and they began to catch animals again and were no longer starving." Tagaaq breathed in a little. "I am named after my mother's little brother who passed away the day my mother became blind."

Pitu did not speak. The story astounded him every time he heard it. Tagaaq's mother was not only a saviour, but a sacrifice. Even though he had told the story over a hundred times in his lifetime, the emotion it brought to Tagaaq remained a strong surge. "You see, Piturniq"—Tagaaq rubbed his eyes once more—"I am a reincarnation of him. I have brilliant eyesight because my mother gifted it to me. I can hear the wind and see the lights of the spirits because she sacrificed part of her power to save him, to lend to him, and it came to live within me, because of my name. So, she did save her little brother, do you understand?"

Finally, Pitu spoke in a hoarse voice. "Yes, I understand."

"Our village never quite needed a shaman after my mother passed away. She still lives without her body, and she still protects us." Tagaaq grew silent for a moment. He gazed at the blueness of the melting inlet in front of them. Pitu studied him. His eyes were those of a wise elder, with white circles around the irises, and they were glassy with his unshed tears. When Tagaaq looked down at the stone man he held in his hand, Pitu followed his gaze. "This is for you, young leader."

Tagaaq extended his hand to give the figurine to him. Pitu took hold of it and examined the carving. It was a fine piece of craftsmanship. Something about it made Pitu vow to himself that he would not let another human hand touch this little hunter. He thanked Tagaaq.

"Do you wonder why I told you that story?" Tagaaq asked.

Pitu grimaced for a moment in thought. He wrinkled his nose in dissent. "It is a story I have heard many times, Uncle."

"Yes, I do enjoy telling it." Tagaaq laughed

lightly. "However, there is a reason this time. You may not be very fond of that reason."

Pitu did not reply, choosing instead to simply wait for the answer.

"I do believe that you have the gifts my mother had," Tagaaq said. "I believe there is much darkness in your future."

"I don't understand."

"Piturniq, the Great Hunter, the young leader." Tagaaq laughed lightly. "You are a strong young man; a wise one, too. I think it is because you are to become a shaman."

"A shaman?" Pitu was shocked. "But you just said we don't need a shaman."

"Maybe not right now," Tagaaq said, "but my mother's spirit lives as long as I do. And I have grown very old. Her spirit withers with each passing year. Today, at the top of that mountain, I heard the spirits as they praised you."

"What would it mean for me to become a shaman?"

"You will live a normal life." Tagaaq smiled. "You will be a leader, and you will have to take counsel with the spirits when need be."

"I still don't understand."

"It grows late." Tagaaq patted Pitu's shoulder. "We have a long journey ahead of us. Once we reach our summer home we will speak of this further."

"Yes," Pitu said, his shoulders tense. "Okay."

"Perhaps you should not speak of this to your mother for now," Tagaaq said as they walked back to camp. "I know that she is very sensitive about this topic."

Pitu agreed. He would not speak of this to anyone. The news shook his whole being. His whole life, this camp had never needed a shaman. It was an indulgence when the shamans told their stories during the celebrations in the qaggiq, but he thought of them only as storytellers and travellers. He'd heard of their stories, listened to their songs, but he had never seen their power.

That night, when he fell asleep next to his little brother, Tagaaq's words stuck in his head: *I believe there is much darkness in your future.*

6

Summary

*I*t took two more weeks for the group of twenty-four to reach their ideal summer camp. The foundations of their *qarmait*, sod houses made of stone and moss, were already set up from the previous summer, with enormous bones of bowhead whale placed on the rooftops. The women went off to gather moss to stick into crevices between the rocks as insulation. Men began to set their camps, tying the dogs up around the outside of their houses, resting caribou hides over the whalebone roofs, or setting up the caribou and sealskin tents. Children went off to play among the lichen-covered boulders and rolling hillsides, with their mothers worriedly calling after them, "Don't wander too far or the *inugarulliit* will get you!" warning the little ones of the mischievous and violent dwarves that prey on those who disturb their homes.

The summer camp was along a wide peninsula. At the top a low hill was a collection of inuksuit, marking the area as a good hunting and gathering spot. The beach was gravelly with small rocks and sand. The hillside was covered in patches of snow, with moss and lichen throughout. Once the sun stopped setting and hung in the sky twenty-four hours a day, the snow would melt and reveal berries and the buds of purple flowers. The houses and tents were set in a flat area in the middle of the hill, a stretch that was laid out almost perfectly for human habitation. The group had been camping here for four summers in a row, but soon they would be in search of a new summer home. The animals would adapt and move on. The people had to be just as adaptable. This nomadic way of life also ensured that the earth would replenish itself.

Natsivaq looked at Pitu pointedly, nodding toward the top of the hill. Some men were already headed up to the top. Pitu lay down his belongings, which were wrapped in the hide of a caribou. The two men began their walk up the hill in silence. There was never much need for conversation with Natsivaq. He was good company in that way, and an even better hunting partner.

At the crest of the hill, the men began removing large mounds of rocks in the centre. The hard work uncovered the smell of *igunaq*, fermented walrus meat. Pitu felt the saliva form in his mouth as he thought of having the tasty meat. A hearty meal would be had this evening. His stomach clenched; he was getting hungry from all the work they'd done that day. The snow and ice were melting quickly; they had to hop over large cracks in the ice, pushing the sleds out of ditches that were hard to see until it was too late. Each man partnered with another and took a skin bag of meat for his family, and began the walk back down the hill.

After giving the meat to his mother, Pitu left the house again to go to the beach. The skeletons of qajait were set on top of racks made of driftwood and bone. Some boats were larger than others. The smaller ones were meant to carry only an individual, while the larger boats could carry many members of a family in the hull—a tight fit that was sometimes necessary. Counting the frames, Pitu could see about eight. He went to the one he had inherited when his father died and inspected it for any damage caused throughout the winter. There was a large break on a plank of the driftwood, but otherwise nothing else seemed to be wrong. Other members of the group were less fortunate. Some boats had fallen off the racks over the winter and frozen to the ground. Some had been trampled by passing animals. Then there were the boats that were missing altogether: they'd been taken or had blown far away and were lost forever.

They laid the qajait back on top of the racks, and off they went to their respective stone houses, where their wives or mothers were already lighting their lamps and cutting up meat for their children.

Pitu went to help Anaana without a thought, cutting little pieces for Atiq while he fidgeted around with unending energy. The young boy pawed at Anaana, pushed at Arnaapik, and jumped on Pitu, which resulted in Pitu slicing his index finger open with his knife.

"*NUKARLAALUK!* Stupid little brother!" Pitu shouted in reaction more than anger. Atiq bellowed in return, tears already forming in his eyes. Anaana giggled to herself while Arnaapik ignored them all, grabbing her *ulu* and cutting pieces of meat for herself. Pitu scolded Atiq with a strike to the head and made his way outside to wash his bloody hand off with snow. His little brother cried remorselessly.

Only a few people were left outside. Men stood by their boats, still inspecting the damage. Children played tirelessly, either on the hill or on the ice. Passersby laughed when they saw Pitu cleaning his small wound, no doubt because they had heard the outburst and guessed what had happened. Anaana came a moment later with a piece of meat and a hunk of moss. He took the meat wordlessly and scarfed it down. He'd done a fair bit of work today, and the taste of the igunaq suddenly awakened his hunger. Anaana tended to the wound, grabbing a bit of snow and wrapping his hand in the moss dressing. She held his hand aloft to ease the flow of blood and pressure.

"Perhaps soon the boy will learn," Anaana said conversationally.

Pitu only nodded. He was suddenly exhausted. He said, "I'm hungry."

Anaana laughed. Their relationship had rebalanced itself over the past month. They were close again, able to speak as mother and son. She was tiny—almost a whole head shorter than he was—and her body was growing frail. He wished that he could not see her aging. It made him think too much of his late father.

She looked away from his hand as someone approached from behind him. Anaana smiled. Pitu turned around to see Saima holding a length of string. Pitu was abashed. Why was she here? Did she hear him yell at Atiq? How embarrassing. He didn't want her to think he was still suffering from outbursts and rudeness. She said, "I brought this to tie up the dressing."

Anaana didn't say a word, she only handed Pitu's wrapped hand to Saima and left them alone. Saima removed the moss to look at the cut. A wide smile broke the guarded expression on her face and she laughed. "You made all that fuss for this little cut?"

"There was no fuss," Pitu reacted quickly. "I'm too manly to fuss."

Saima grabbed another handful of snow, rubbed it onto the cut once more and then ripped a bit of the moss off. She told Pitu to hold it on the cut while she wrapped the string she had brought and tied a knot to keep it there. "This is unnecessary, Saimaniq," Pitu said.

"No one wants our Great Hunter to lose a finger." She smiled with warmth. The sight of it almost blinded Pitu. "And I am sure our Great Hunter does not want to seem weak for all the noise he made for this measly little wound?"

"Oh, so you're just making sure that we are all looking good?"

"Among other things." She put a hand on his chest for a brief moment and took it away shyly. "Tagaaq told me to find you. He wants to speak to you."

"Right now?"

"No," she teased, a smirk replacing her warm smile with mischief. "Your stomach is rumbling too loudly. No one would be able to hear anything. Go and eat, then sleep. You can see him in the morning. Don't hurt yourself."

It seemed that Saima was already looking after him, like she would as his wife. She began to walk away. Pitu had a subtle urge to just grab her, to keep her with him and to promise her the world ... but a pang in his stomach made it feel as if the organ began to eat itself, so he made his way back to the sod house his family was in. Though they seemed to be on friendly terms again, Pitu still wanted to make it up to Saima, to convince her that he was not a bad person. Once he finished eating and his siblings were fast asleep, he asked his mother how he could achieve this.

Anaana grinned knowingly. "What have you done to prove this to her so far?"

"I apologized for how I acted," Pitu said. "And I promised not to be like that ever again."

Anaana waved him off with amusement. "I am not the one you should speak to about this. Talk to Natsivaq when you have matters of the heart."

Pitu's face reddened when he realized what he'd done. Discussing this topic with his mother was inappropriate, especially when she was an elder. Anaana was not offended, if anything she found it hilarious. She laughed quietly so as not to wake the kids. Anaana called him a silly boy.

His embarrassment soon amused him, too. He shed his clothing and crawled into bed next to his little brother. Atiq was sprawled wide, his mouth hanging open since his nose held too much mucus to breathe through. He snored like he was a sleeping walrus. Pitu moved the boy's limbs over and lay down on his back, falling asleep quickly and soundly with exhaustion and the comfort of a full stomach and a happy mother.

In the morning, Pitu left for Tagaaq's sod house. A growing uneasiness developed in his stomach. The thought of their conversation only a couple of weeks ago swept into his mind. So, this was it. This was when he would find out what Tagaaq had truly intended for him to learn.

Tagaaq and his wife sat outside their house with other members of the camp. Pitu sat down next to his puukuluk. She leaned over and kissed him on the cheek, handing over her youngest child, a baby girl, into his arms. She went off to find a private spot to pee. The elders were telling stories, as they normally do, and all those surrounding them were laughing. The cool air was calming and peaceful, and little snow buntings were singing songs. It was a lovely gathering. Unfortunately, as Pitu sat there with the infant on his lap listening to the elders, he could not find any focus. He thought of the words about darkness that Tagaaq had said. They'd been running through his mind every day for the past two weeks, keeping him up at night.

Pitu sat with them until Tagaaq finally stood up and gestured for him to follow. He gave the baby back to his puukuluk and caught up to Tagaaq. Those they left behind began conversations centred on the elder and his protege, each person trying to come up with an answer as to what the two would discuss that day.

The first thing that Tagaaq said was, "Are you well rested?"

"Yes," Pitu replied.

"I have somewhere in mind for us to talk, although it will be a bit of a long walk." Tagaaq smiled. "We will also try to catch some birds."

The sun was high in the sky when they finally stopped to rest next to a stream of fresh water. They'd been walking for hours, with two ptarmigans each to show for it. The elder brought out a cup made from sealskin, the fur shaved off with a knife, to fill it with water from the stream. Pitu did the same. They sat quietly for a few moments.

"It seems my son has grown jealous of you," Tagaaq began conversationally.

Pitu didn't think much of Tagaaq's son, Qajaarjuaq. He was Natsivaq's age, but remained unmarried, as far as Pitu could tell. Qajaarjuaq was a decent hunter and provided most of his catches to his sisters' families and the elderly in the camp, since Tagaaq caught plenty as well. He travelled a lot, going mainly between Iglulik and Tununiq, where they usually wintered. This summer, Qajaarjuaq had decided to stay. There were rumours that he was staying in protest to the camp's decision for Pitu to become the next leader, thinking that the role belonged to Tagaaq's descendants rather than a random young hunter. Pitu shrugged, which made Tagaaq smile.

"Being a leader is difficult, Piturniq," Tagaaq said. "Have you thought of that?"

"Yes," Pitu replied. "All the time."

"Qajaarjuaq thinks it would be more appropriate for him to lead."

"I am aware of that," Pitu said, as he shrugged again. "Maybe it is more appropriate. I am still young."

"Age doesn't matter," Tagaaq said. "Only your ability and discipline. My son has no discipline. He cannot stay still for long. He is a bad husband ... he has many women in his life, many children, but no one he takes care of."

"He takes care of his sisters," Pitu chimed in. "And the elders ... He has the potential to be a leader."

Tagaaq chuckled. "Yes, when he is here he seems to be a good man, doesn't he? Yet he has two wives who live together in Iglulik and raise his two sons and three daughters, but he does not stay there to teach his sons the ways of men and hunters. His wives are poor and mistreated, the charity of the village ... yet he stays here."

"Perhaps he should move them here?" Pitu suggested.

"Do you wish not to be a leader anymore, Piturniq?" Tagaaq asked. "You try to defend Qajaarjuaq. Have I frightened you with what I told you all those weeks ago?"

"I am confused, Uncle," Pitu said. "You spoke of darkness. That is what frightens me."

"I do sense darkness in your future." Tagaaq nodded. "Let me tell you a story. When I was your age, I went to a qaggiq far, far away. My mother was asked to go there by a hunter named Tunu. He was the largest man I have ever seen ... yes, yes, like Arnatsiaq, only larger ... and he travelled to Ikpiarjuk seeking my mother to tell her of a shaman from a large island in the east. So, my mother told us that we were to travel there for the return of the sun.

"After weeks of travelling, we made it to the island where this shaman, whose name I have long forgotten, lived. A qaggiq so large it could fit every person in this camp and every person in their camp was built in the centre of a long expanse of clear and flat ground. It was made from clear ice, and behind it was an open lake bereft of ice.

"My mother brought me with her when she went to greet the shaman she had heard so much about. I guided her to the iglu we were told was his. Upon entering, we saw the face of the most beautiful woman I had ever seen. She had long black hair braided in two, and perfect blue tattoos to show off her womanhood and enhance her beauty. She breastfed a newborn child, while singing a lullaby to a small toddler. When she saw my mother and me, she smiled ... I fell in love with her instantly. Unfortunately, she was already married to this mysterious shaman we had come so far to see.

"He, on the other hand, was not very beautiful. He was a skinny man with a beard and long black hair. He had a parka of solid white, the most pristine parka I had ever seen. He invited us in, having heard of who my mother was and recognizing her blind eyes. He held her hand as they spoke.

"I wish I could tell you his name, but it left my memory a long time ago. He was the best shaman that ever lived. He cheated death many times and healed many sick. He travelled to the bottom of the ocean and combed the hair of the great and vengeful sea goddess, Nuliajuk. He flew in the sky to catch birds or jump across rivers. He could transform into a wolf to search for food or save himself in dire circumstances. During the celebrations on that island, I saw him get stabbed with a harpoon in his stomach. Women cried and men shouted. The harpoon protruded from his back ... I saw his blood ... yet when he pulled it out and took off his parka, there was no wound on his torso, only a small patch of red and raw skin."

Pitu shivered at this story. He had heard of shamans who could do those acts of true power, but he had never heard of any single shaman being able to do all of them. Tagaaq continued, "After that, we went to see him twice more. He lived very far away and the journey was hard. The last time I saw him, his beautiful wife was pregnant with their fourth child. He was happy, healthy ... they were a beautiful family.

"Shortly after seeing them last, we heard the news that his wife and children had died unexpectedly. The shaman vanished. No one heard from him or saw him ever again."

Pitu waited for more, but Tagaaq had stopped speaking and was crying silently to himself. Tears ran down his face. The elder sipped the water from his cup and breathed heavy breaths of grief. The story was emotional and eerie. Pitu felt something, like the power of the story was unfolding inside of him. There was a lump in his throat as he stayed silent next to the old man.

Finally, Tagaaq continued, "The darkness I sense in you, Piturniq, feels like the tragedy of the shaman's family. It is frightening to feel this around you."

"I do not understand, Uncle," Pitu replied. "Am I cursed to repeat this tragedy with my own family?"

"No, I do not think so," Tagaaq took another long sip of water, finishing what was in his cup. "I think that you must find the lost shaman. What happened to his family ... it has shrouded and hidden him for decades. In order for you to learn your power, you must find him so that he can teach you."

"How would I find a man who has been lost for decades?" Pitu asked. "How do you know that he is still alive? He must have died many years ago."

"He is not dead." Tagaaq's tone was firm. "That is all the spirits can tell me. The only one with the ability to find this man is you, Piturniq the Great Hunter."

7

Powers

The summer continued on. The days grew warm and bright, the ice in the inlet slowly breaking up, melting, moving in and out. There were caribou and seal aplenty, and men travelled great lengths in search of muskoxen. Women throat-sang to soothe the babies on their backs. Young children picked berries and birds' eggs with their grandmothers' guidance. Young women sewed new boots while their mothers busied themselves with making new clothes for the young children who grew too fast for the clothing to fit for long.

When the ice left and there was open water as far as the eye could see, the hunters left on their boats daily in search of seals, walruses, and whales. They paddled for long hours of the day, until they caught something to bring back home. As they leisurely paddled back to their little camp with a seal or two harnessed to their boat, the sunlight dimmed slightly, and they sang about their hunting trip or about legendary hunters and deities.

Each day, Pitu would go to see Tagaaq, and the elder would tell him another story, mostly stories not as emotional as the one about the lost shaman. Pitu's mother was always happy to see her son; no longer was she wary when people spoke of him as the new leader-to-be. When others praised him as the Great Hunter, his mother praised louder. When others, such as Qajaarjuaq, pointed out his youth, Pitu's mother laughed and pointed out how old they were.

Saima no longer seemed to be mad at him. In fact, she often ran to him when he returned from a hunting trip, and she would inspect the animals he had caught. If he had any birds, he would give them to her because he knew that her mother liked them. Over the summer, she was getting tattoos engraved into her skin. On her forehead was a thin double V, the larger of the two going ever-so-slightly between her brows, the other smaller and laid inside of it. The first time he saw Saima's tattoos, Pitu could feel heat rushing through his body. Saima was beautiful, and he was going to be her husband.

One day, a group of boats could be seen in the distance. There were five men in qajait that were three times the length of their bodies. When they reached the beach, they hopped out and helped women out of the hulls. The women appeared to be dizzy and blinded by the sunlight. These were the people from Iglulik coming to look for wives.

Pitu followed Tagaaq and went to greet the new arrivals and assist them in securing their boats to the racks. Pitu found Arnatsiaq and shook his hand. The man turned to the others and said, "This is the boy I spoke of!"

After first being introduced to Tagaaq, the men and women from Iglulik all came forward to shake Pitu's hand. The gesture was strange. He took his discomfort in stride, remembering that one of Tagaaq's lessons was that he would never be truly comfortable with the way people addressed him when he became a leader.

The women seemed happy and excited to have arrived, and the men likewise. Each sought to catch up with cousins and aunts and uncles they hadn't seen for months or years. Pitu's oldest brother, Masik, had arrived, too, along with his cousin Aapak, a young woman with a face full of tattoos to show her maturity and that she was ready for marriage. Pitu hugged them, happy to see familiar faces among the new arrivals. He brought them to his family's sod house to see Anaana.

Masik had moved to a camp near Iglulik years ago to marry a young woman. Usually, it was customary for the new wife to move and live with the husband and his family, but Pitu's family was quite well off, full of strong hunters at the time of the marriage. Masik's wife's family, however, had just lost one of her brothers, so they needed a strong hunter. Pitu's oldest sibling decided that it would make more sense, and serve more purpose, if he went to Iglulik with his lovely wife, and helped to take care of the woman's elderly parents.

Aapak was a funny girl. She was shy and quiet, but once she felt comfortable, she was loud and silly. When she saw Anaana, Aapak ran to her great-aunt and hugged her quietly. She then said hello to Pitu's siblings, and they all sat outside the sod house with a pot of water for boiling goose eggs over a fire. Everyone except the children was there to welcome her: Pitu, Anaana, Arnaapik, Natsivaq and Puukuluk, their children, and Pitu's two older sisters. Aapak was quiet for a moment, stealing glances at Pitu in odd moments. Anaana sat next to Masik, a smile plastered across her face. She was a woman who was proud of all her children. Aapak sat on Anaana's other side; Pitu sat across from the three of them.

"Aapak, you have grown so beautiful," Anaana said. She touched Aapak's amauti. "Did you sew this yourself?"

"Yes, Great-Aunt," Aapak replied. "I was sewing a lot for my mother, but now that my brother is married there is less work for her, so she thought I should come here to find a husband."

Puukuluk spoke with her gentle voice. "There are many good hunters here who need a wife. You will find someone soon."

Aapak looked up and stared at Pitu for a moment, making him uncomfortable. Since she arrived, she had been looking at him like she expected him to be the one to marry her. He would have to tell her that he had already found a wife.

As if she had known he was thinking of her, Saima came to say hello to Aapak. The girls had been friends as children, when Aapak and her family would come to visit. She hugged Aapak and spoke of how happy she was to see her again. Aapak was happy, too. Saima took a hold of her hand, and told her to come for a short walk with her. Anaana said it was okay, and the girls left, giggling like children.

Pitu could only guess what they would talk about, but he thought he might be mentioned at least once or twice. He looked all over the camp to see reunited families and relatives. Pitu was happy that Masik had decided to be the one to escort Aapak here. They hadn't seen each other for years. Before now, the last time Masik had travelled to see them was when their father had died. Pitu remembered Masik saying how strange it was to be there without his father, how different it felt. Their father had been an important man. He had raised three excellent hunters, and was about to begin teaching Atiq the ways of the land and animals before his untimely death. He also raised three lovely daughters, and spoiled them more than he should have, but the girls had grown into strong women, two of whom married and had children, while Arnaapik would take care of Anaana and Atiq until it was her time for marriage.

A reunion among the children of Inuuja and Ujarasuk, Pitu's parents, was long overdue. They told funny stories and laughed. Pitu's older siblings teased him about his nickname, "the Great Hunter," but they also praised him for his new role in the camp as a leader. Pitu remained silent, blushing at the banter. He still hadn't told anyone that he was now to become a shaman, because he was still frightened by the thought. He wondered what their reactions would be if they had known that was the case.

People came and went to visit Pitu's mother. Anaana had grown up in the Iglulik area and the

people who came to see her were nieces and nephews or the children and grandchildren of her childhood friends. They were named after people in her life such as her late grandparents, parents, and brothers and sisters. Anaana would smile and greet the visitors as if they were her actual relatives, being respectful of those named after her grandparents, or being playful with those named after her sisters. She cried small tears of happiness at each visitor.

Once things had settled down, and it was agreed that Aapak would be staying with his family (Masik had brought his own tent, so it wouldn't be crowded), Pitu went to check on the puppies that would grow to be his dog team. The little huskies wrestled with each other and ran back and forth, jumping up and barking and howling. They were not so little anymore, actually. At just over five months old, the puppies were already almost fully grown and were ready for their training to pull sleds as soon as fall arrived with snow. As the puppies played, one in particular ran up to him to lick his legs and hands. Pitu bent down to pet the puppy, and recognized it to be the black-and-white one he had picked up and kept in his pocket when they were travelling. He had named her Miki, "small one," because she had been the smallest of the litter, but now he could see that she had grown to be one of the biggest dogs of the pack.

He threw pieces of seal meat to the other dogs that were playing around, and fed Miki from his hand. It seemed that being hauled in his pocket had made her fond of him. Pitu felt the same; she was his favourite of the huskies, and her one brown eye and one blue eye made him like her more. Though the huskies were working dogs, Miki was loving and affectionate. He knew that soon, Miki would become his lead dog.

"You're the only girl I need," Pitu murmured to Miki.

Every night, Pitu dreamt of following the fox toward the strange island of sunlight in the middle of the sea. Sometimes it was a hot summer day and he was paddling in his qajaq, sweating from the heat of the light bearing down on him. Other times it was amid the torrential winds and blowing snow of a blizzard, where he had to cover his face to protect it as he stayed focused on the fox's footprints that quickly faded in the snow. Never did he reach that island—until one night, he fell asleep and saw an elder standing alone on the beach. Pitu did not recognize the old man scowling at him.

Throughout the summer, Pitu proved to be the great hunter he was told over and over again that he was. He guided the hunters to wildlife, his harpoon was first to strike a beluga, he caught birds with a perfectly measured throw of a pebble with a slingshot, and he showed restraint when he had enough food to eat at home. When not hunting, he created tools to aid his hunting and everyday life, making knives from sharpening the bones of the animals he caught into blades, creating harnesses for his dogs to pull the sled that held his supplies, sewing and blowing up a sealskin to use as a buoy when hunting for sea mammals. He gifted his extra food to elders of the village and those he respected. The other hunters no longer teased him, for he had grown into a far more skilled man than they all were.

As he grew into his new role in the village, his ability became far more prominent. His sight was unmatched; he could spot animals from farther away than anyone else, and his aim was never off. Patience was an extension of his mind. His jealousy withdrew, his acceptance of circumstance unfurled with ease. His wisdom remained intact and came easily to him when he spoke with others. Soon, the people of his camp did not think of him as a young hunter, but as a new leader. Pitu had grown into a man he felt his father would be proud of.

It was a foggy day when Pitu went out alone in a qajaq. The other hunters argued that it was unwise to go with such low visibility and no hunting companion. Normally, Pitu would agree; to go out into the fog was an invitation to get lost, and that ultimately meant death. However, on that day, he had a thought stuck in his mind, an instinct telling him that he needed to be alone in this mist. He told the men to trust that he would be back soon.

He went off into the thick clouds. The water was motionless with the lack of wind. When he was utterly alone, far enough away that the sounds of the camp were silenced and the envelopment of the fog hid him from them, he could sense everything that he could not see. The animals in the ocean beneath his boat swam fast as they enjoyed the calm sea, the birds flew in a lost haze, the air was tired from long journeys through the sky and across the lands as it gusted to and fro ... today it wanted to rest.

Everything out here was an extension of Pitu's soul. He could feel the berries growing on the hillside just as well as he could feel the wiggle of his toes. His breath was that of the earth and sea. It was satisfying, this realization. He knew, deep in the farthest reaches of his mind, that he belonged exactly where he was— taking care of his family and the camp. His feet were following the path he was always meant to follow.

There is no darkness within me, he thought as he took it all in.

8

Winter

As the ice returned in jagged blocks adjacent to the shoreline, the nomadic Inuit grew restless in their wait for the water to freeze so they could begin their next journey. By midautumn, the camp members had begun to pack up their summer homes and ready themselves for another expedition to a suitable winter spot. The hunters rebuilt their sleds by freezing moss together to make the runners, securing the boards that would hold it all in place. They also secured the qajait back onto their racks, with the thought of those who lost their boats over the last winter.

By the time the ocean had frozen and was safe enough to travel upon, the hills were already covered in white snow. They packed their supplies onto the sleds and got the dogs to start pulling. Pitu had his own sled, with his own dogs finally old enough to start training. The first few days were tough. The dogs tired easily, often meaning that Pitu had to run next to them. Though Pitu had always enjoyed running, the lack of suitable rest grew exhausting, and when he would set the tent for his mother, he'd eat a few bites of seal, or fish, or bear, or caribou, and then fall into a heavy sleep.

Still he dreamt of following the fox. He'd grown familiar enough with it to call it Tiri, the short form of *tiriganniaq*, which only meant "fox." Sometimes in these dreams, he saw the elder that lived on the island. At first, though he did not recognize this man, Pitu thought it was his father trying to teach him a lesson. After the fourth or fifth dream, however, Pitu knew that it was not him. Pitu's father was far too direct to let a dream trouble his son for so long, leaving him confused and unsure of how to move forward.

The days grew easier as the dogs gained new muscle and understood their purpose. They ran efficiently and remained focused. Soon, Pitu only ran when he had to guide the dogs around the bumpy fields of jagged ice and cracks.

Instead of returning to Tununiq, the camp went to an area closer to Iglulik. Tagaaq thought it appropriate to have the new and young wives, who had become homesick, close to their families during their adjustment to their new husbands and in-laws. Pitu suspected it might also have something to do with Qajaarjuaq's abandoned wives. Soon after arriving, the man left for the village and only came back once in a while for brief visits. There were still some men looking for wives, many of them taking an interest in Saima and asking to marry her. Pitu was relieved that Saima's parents remained adamant that she would marry Pitu, but it still made him uneasy. In the back of his mind, he kept thinking that they would change their minds if a man made an offer that her parents would be unable to say no to.

The days were cold and dark, as the sun never rose above the horizon. Instead, the sky was illuminated in a vividly colourful twilight of blues, oranges, and pinks for a few hours at midday. Soon, even that light disappeared for months.

The camp kept busy as ever, hunting and preparing. Newly married couples announced pregnancies, including Pitu's cousin Aapak. She had married a small man who was a skilled hunter, but he was quite a bit older than she was. She did not seem to mind. They were a happy couple.

Pitu asked Natsivaq what he should do so that he could marry Saima. Natsivaq said to wait. When he asked Tagaaq, the elder said the same thing. Pitu wondered if Saima would understand. They were already slightly older than the usual marrying age, and there were certain expectations for them to uphold.

Young couples are supposed to be having children and teaching them to be good hunters and providers, seamstresses and caregivers, which would ensure that life would continue to thrive through the winters in the future.

One day, just before Pitu was preparing for another day of hunting, Saima came to see him as he tied his last piece of equipment onto his qamutiik. Pitu smiled, but it was hard to see anything in the darkness.

"Why haven't you married me yet?" she asked bluntly.

Pitu could feel the embarrassment on his face, and he was briefly grateful for the lack of sunlight. After a moment of silence, he replied, "So, you do want to marry me, ai?"

"Saimaniq, wife of Piturniq the Great Hunter." She pondered this for a moment. "It does sound nice, doesn't it?"

A shiver went down his spine when she said that. Pitu smiled. "I will marry you," he said. "Maybe not today or tomorrow, but I will. I've asked, but my training has to be completed before we can get married."

"Oh." She scowled. "Did you know that someone proposed marriage to me last summer?"

Pitu nodded. He remembered hearing of it from Saima's little brother. Pitu had just returned from the foggy ride in the qajaq he had taken. The young boy ran to him at the beach and spewed the words out. His feeling of peace and resolve quickly evaporated. He ran to Amarualik's sod house and saw only the old man and his wife there. They greeted him with the words, "I told the man that she is already betrothed."

Relief had flooded him then, the peace slowly ebbing in and out. After talking to Saima's parents, he wanted to find his mother to ask when he could marry, but thought it better to ask Natsivaq.

Saima shook her head slightly, as if disappointed.

Pitu touched her arm. "After that, I asked to marry you right away, but Tagaaq said I cannot marry you yet."

He could see her eyes shining with unshed tears.

"I just need you to wait for me, okay, Saimaniq?" Pitu told her. He wanted to lighten the situation. "Saimaniq the Beautiful? No, that's not the right name for you ... Saimaniq the Joker?"

She tightened her lips in a restricted smile.

"I am in love with you," Pitu whispered to her. It was the first time he had said the words aloud. "I will tell the elders that we cannot wait anymore when I return from this hunting trip, okay? I will marry you as soon as I come back."

Saima beamed, a true smile this time. Then she wrapped her arms around him in an intimate embrace. "Please catch a seal and return as soon as you can," she said, before she brushed her mouth and nose on his cheek and inhaled softly. She turned away and went back to her iglu.

9

Whiteout

*I*t was as if the animals knew how much Pitu wanted to return to camp, because he could find no tracks or breathing holes. The breathing holes he did find were too dangerous to go near, broken wide open. In the centres of the holes were chunks of ice and seaweed, looking like the hair of a person who had fallen in. The strangest part was that the breathing holes he had caught seals at only a couple of days before were now gone, as if they had never been broken open at all. He searched tirelessly, but to no avail. He could not sense any animals to hunt.

His dog team stopped midstride, staring off into the distance. Their bodies stiffened, noses jutting forward to sniff the air. It took a moment for Pitu to realize that the huskies were doing this out of caution rather than exhaustion. He looked up, dropping his pack, and squinted in order to see through the darkness. There was nothing to see.

The air was dead. The absence of wind making it eerie and silent.

Oh no, Pitu thought. *Blizzard.*

His lead dog let out a sharp bark in warning, and then let out a low and piercing howl. Pitu jumped, dove for his pack, and took out his snow knife. Hopefully he had enough time to build a shelter while it was still calm before the storm. Pitu was glad that he had chosen this path for his journey as he carved into the snow to make the blocks for an impromptu iglu. The snow was hard and solid.

He was about a quarter of the way done when the wind began to pick up. The dogs ran back and forth, urging Pitu to hurry up. About halfway through building the iglu, the intensity of the wind bit into his face. It did not stop him from building the iglu. He continued on.

The dogs barked with impatience. Pitu looked up to where the sound came from, except the dogs were not visible. The wind blew the loose snow into the air. It swirled around in a dance, sticking to Pitu's lashes and playing with his vision. All he could see were the hazy shapes of his dogs running away, hauling his sled full of tools and emergency food. Then, they were gone, and he was left alone.

No.

He took a step forward and the world seemed to open up beneath his feet. He fell onto his back as he slipped on nothing, toppling over onto a patch of ice.

The snow had suddenly been swept away by the wind. Trying to get to his feet, he slipped again, falling onto his front. Pitu caught his fall with his arms outstretched. His *kamiik* found no grip on the ice that surrounded him. It was the palest shade of blue, so thick that the water underneath wasn't visible.

The half-built iglu was gone. His dogs had left him. The only thing left was the snow knife Pitu held in his hand and his harpoon that lay an arm's length away. The rest of his gear was gone: his dried and frozen food, stone lamp and bowl, the sinew and ivory needle. All he had was his hunting utensils, nothing particularly practical. If he caught something, he'd have to wrap it up in its skin, tying it up with the limbs and carrying it. Or he would have to eat what he could and leave the rest behind, which was an utter waste and an incredibly shameful thing to do. The mere thought of it all exhausted him.

Pitu crawled toward his harpoon and gripped it tightly. The wind was still roaring around him in an angry swirl. It seemed that the wind was a living creature, howling in rage and turmoil. Pitu's ears rang with the sound. He was growing more and more afraid as the wind swept him over the flat and smooth ice.

He'd never seen ice so flat, no cracks caused by the tides, no jagged pieces jutting up into a terrifying landscape, no holes for seals to breathe through or polar bears to hunt by. It was smooth as far as he could see. Granted, he could not see very far.

Hours seemed to pass.

Pitu lay on the ice, huddled into a ball, clinging to his tools. He thought of his dogs, especially Miki. There was nothing else to think of, other than his occasional remembrance of how horrified he was. He tried to think of home and his mother and Saima, but that brought only bad feelings, not comfort. The strength of the wind was blowing him around in all directions, toying with him and terrorizing him.

When he finally opened his eyes again, they were sore from being shut so tightly for such a long period of time. The sky above was a pure and unfaltering shade of grey that hurt Pitu's eyes, like an overcast day in spring. After several moments, he gathered enough strength to push himself up into a seated position. He was no longer on an endless expanse of smooth ice; instead he was now sitting at the bottom of a hill in the middle of the day. The air was cool, but not bracing. Everywhere he looked, there was white snow. The sea ice he'd been blown across was adjacent to him. As far as he could see, there were no signs of life, no tracks in the snow. Even the air felt dead, as the strong winds had completely vanished. The things that would be typical of a shoreline, like tidal ice, rocks peeking through the snow, meandering fox tracks, and constant wind, were not present, making everything seem smooth and unnatural.

He looked around some more, searching but finding no trace of his dogs. His heartbeat quickened. Although the landscape was vastly unnerving, there was also a sense of vague familiarity, like it was his world shown to him through the stillness of a lake. A reflection of the truth. He could see peaks in the distance, and the hill he sat upon was a part of a range of ancient, weather-softened mountains, not unlike the ones his village camped along.

"*Qimmiit!*" Pitu shouted into the strange land. "Come here! Dogs!"

There were no distant barks or howls in answer, just the echo of his voice. Pitu continued to shout for several moments, more out of confusion and disbelief than the thought that they might hear him. The last time he had glimpsed the huskies, they'd been running away with his sled full of gear. They were long gone by now, probably back at camp. Anaana would be worried, sending all the hunters in the camp and in nearby Iglulik to search for him. It could take days for him to return, and he was afraid to start a journey when he did not know where he was. What if he chose the wrong way and started a journey in the opposite direction of his camp? He wouldn't know anything until he saw another person.

He thought solemnly of the promise he'd made to Saima. He worried that she might think he had left and disappeared on purpose because he was too afraid of marrying her. He quickly dismissed the ridiculous thought. He'd been told too many times this past summer that the whole village knew he wanted her to be his wife. *There's no way Saima would think I left to hide from my commitments*, he thought. It could take weeks until he could explain to her what had happened, but he believed that she would wait for him.

After sitting at the bottom of the hillside for what felt like hours, shouting until his throat was raw and sore, Pitu finally got to his feet. In either hand he held the snow knife and harpoon, using the latter as a walking stick. There was no way the dogs wouldn't have heard him, unless he had travelled farther than the wind could possibly have taken him. Pitu knew that there were many things wrong about the whole situation, but he still refused to believe it.

Once he began to move and walk up the hill, Pitu's senses slowly returned to him. The strangeness of the land around seemed to be speaking to him. Pitu felt that he was no longer in the same land that he had been in. The feeling he had felt last summer in the fog was gone. No longer was he filled with peace and purpose. Now, he was enveloped in hostility. He was not at home here. The thought brought an ache to his chest. He thought of Saima, of how close they had been only this morning. The thoughts overwhelmed him and he chose not to dwell on them any longer.

A gust of wind blew over the hill. It carried the sound of a wailing woman.

Pitu started up the hill at a quick pace, more out of excitement at the prospect of seeing another person and finding answers than out of concern for why the woman might be crying.

At the crest of the hill, he saw three women huddled together on another expanse of ice, this one more normal looking than the one he had just slid across for what seemed to be miles and miles. Jagged boulders of ice jutted out vertically as signs of the ocean's tides. The women were just a bit farther than the field of ice boulders, staring down into an open crack before them. Another gust of wind swept over him, and Pitu could hear the pathetic crying again.

He made his way down the hillside, calling out to the women. The wind would not carry his words toward them. Pitu walked as quickly as he could without wearing down his energy. When he reached the pillars of ice sticking out of the frozen water, the looming figures towered over him. The ice seemed to cast imaginary shadows underneath their scrutinizing gaze, but in the bland light, it was impossible to truly see the dark shapes the shadows would form. The feeling lingered, though, that there was something terrifying about these jagged figures, some breath of life hiding in their cracks.

I never felt so small, Pitu thought. Not even next to the mountains they went to hunt by in the summer, not even when he paddled the qajaq on great expanses of open water, nor at the sight of the huge bowhead whales in the sea. The beauty of those things far outweighed the formidable danger they could entail. These towering hunks of ice were alien, sharp, and terrible. Pitu felt like they were the ghosts of evil men, taunting him as he hiked through. With the wind carrying the wailing cries of the women through the sharp passage, the place was nightmarish. He sped through the narrow spaces between each formation, a hopeless need to leave the area propelling him forward. He felt the prickles of fright on the back of his neck, the cold sweat coming from his skin. He stumbled through, jumping over dark cracks in which he felt he could hear the breaths of a thousand drowning victims. The ice cast shadows over the path and he had to squint before he could keep manoeuvring his way through, twisting away from the sharp edges.

He slipped a few times before he made his way out. Looking back briefly, Pitu expected to see something like a shadow of darkness on the path he'd just left. He was sure he felt the presence of a malevolent entity within the huddled ice. And yet, he could see that there was nothing. The contorted columns of ice were still and unwavering.

Pitu called out to the women again. They were only ten paces away from each other now. The three women went rigid, their backs straightening, their shabby amautiit jostling what they carried in their pouches. He continued his way toward them, but their wailing had ceased. The oddness of the situation made him hesitate—the terror from his journey through the ice still making his stomach turn, his heart pound, and his skin prickle.

"Ai," Pitu cautiously called out again. He was standing only two or three strides away now.

One of the women turned to look at him.

Pitu stepped back in instant horror, dropping his weapons in shock. It wasn't a woman, he realized instantly. The stories he had been told as a child about playing on the ice alone sprang to memory. He was looking at a *qallupilluq*: a creature that steals lone children.

All three of them swirled around to look at him. Large, bulbous eyes, like those of a fish, bulged out of their faces; their mouths were black holes filled with sharp teeth. The taut skin that clung tightly to their bones was a pallid shade of grey, resembling a drowned body. They wore amautiit that were covered in algae, the hems stripping off, showing their thin arms and legs, their knobby joints. They didn't wear kamiik on their feet, which looked more like flippers.

The three qallupilluit shrieked a piercing noise into Pitu's ears. He leaped back as the closest one swiped a webbed hand with long, sharp claws at his body. The screams coming out of their mouths disoriented him. He fell to his knees, clamping his mitted hands over his ears.

One of the qallupilluit jumped on top of him, the scent of seaweed reaching his nose. He felt the slimy curl of it on his face. Their hair ... their hair was made of seaweed.

The qallupilluq was slight, weighing barely more than a feather, but she had incredible strength in her grip. Her sharp claws dug into his shoulders, her feet—or flippers—pierced into his legs. The screeches coming from her throat were making him go deaf.

Pitu's stomach convulsed. Their shrieks and appearance and scent were making him feel sick. He felt one of the creature's claws cut through his cheek. The slick feeling of blood flowing made his head spin. The qallupilluq on top of him made a sound of disgust and jumped off. He took the opportunity to start crawling away.

Only when he saw his own blood reddening the snow did his stomach convulse hard enough that he vomited. He retched onto the snow until nothing else would come out. The shrieking suddenly stopped.

He looked up to see them observing him. They crouched in a grotesque fashion with their knees turned outward, their curled backs looking ancient and broken. One of the qallupilluit pointed a long, bony finger at him, and in a hoarse voice, asked, "Are you alive?"

Pitu did not respond. The dialect was ancient, but he understood it.

The creatures whispered to each other. Pitu slowly began to regain control over his body. He clenched his hands together over and over again, the movement and concentration calming him, distracting him. He stood up from his position on his hands and knees, getting back to his feet. Though he felt woozy, he wanted to face the qallupilluit with dignity.

One of the qallupilluit, the one in the middle, seemed to be the leader. She growled at the others and addressed Pitu again. "Did you come to steal our babies?"

They didn't wait for him to answer. Instead, all three leaped forward to attack him. Pitu suddenly remembered his weapons. The qallupilluit did not seem to have noticed that the harpoon was on the ground next to their flipper-feet. When they leaped, it was left in the open. Pitu dove for it while the three creatures were midair. He grasped it with a definite grip, readjusted it for aiming, and threw it with all his strength at the qallupilluq in the middle, the one who had spoken to him.

It seemed as though time had stopped as the harpoon sailed through the air. The qallupilluit had their backs to Pitu now, unaware of the harpoon flying toward them. Pitu stared at it, willing it toward his target.

Two of the creatures landed on their feet; one fell into a heap on the ice. The harpoon stood out stiffly from the back of its neck. There was a moment of surprised silence. With horror that mirrored Pitu's, the qallupilluit watched as the life drained out of their kin. The two, aghast and now frightened, straightened from their crouching stances.

"*Nanijauniaravit*," said one in a horrifying whisper. "You'll be found."

The two ran into the trail through the frozen shards of ice that Pitu had just passed through. Pitu shivered, the words finding a way to penetrate his spine and crawl into his mind, momentarily paralyzing him there. He closed his eyes against tears that were beginning to well up. His blood was running through his veins in a terrified frenzy. He knew that this was something he had had to do, he had had no choice, but there were too many thoughts going through his mind. He had just encountered a creature of myth—he had just killed one.

A sudden thought slammed him back from his fear, though the thought was no less dreadful, perhaps more so. He made his way over toward the dead creature in front of him. Pitu warily touched the back of the qallupilluq's amauti. Under his hand, there was no mistaking the solid curve of children in the pouch.

More sickness was forming in his stomach. Pitu didn't want to see them, he didn't want to see what had become of the children that were stolen by the creatures. With courage he did not think he possessed, Pitu opened the hood of the amauti, disturbed to see the two small children in the pouch.

One was a boy, his skin gone blue from asphyxiation and drowning. The little boy must have been three or four. He still wore the caribou snowsuit that his maternal guardian had made for him. The child was shrunken and frozen, dead.

The other child was a girl, slightly older than

the boy, but she was not dead. Instead, she was transforming. The child shied away from him, from the light. Her eyes were almost normal, her hair was almost normal, but her skin was scaly in certain spots … Pitu could see that she was changing. She was becoming like the qallupilluq that had just attacked Pitu. The little girl cried, her voice still human, her mouth still unchanged by the awful transformation. She was still more human than she was monster.

Pitu didn't know what to do. Should he reach in and help her? The little girl whimpered softly. Her mouth was forming words, but he couldn't hear her gentle voice. "*Hai?*" he asked.

"*Avani,*" she mumbled infinitesimally louder. "Go away."

"I can help you," Pitu said, though he was not sure that was true. "You can come with me. I'm a shaman."

"*Avani!*" she shouted, a bit of anger in her voice. "Go away!"

The little girl began to wail like the qallupilluit had before he came along. Her eyes darkened, looking sinister.

Pitu stumbled away. He pulled the harpoon from the dead qallupilluq's neck and grabbed his knife, which was lying a little ways off. He started walking away, passing the crack in the ice the creatures had been crying over. He glanced at the hole. Inside, there was only darkness, but he thought of the holes in the ice he went by sometimes, broken wide open and dangerous, chunks of ice and frozen seaweed floating at the surface. He couldn't help but imagine his little brother and sister, standing at the edge of one of those holes and peering in, hoping to see a seal, and instead finding bony hands reaching out and grabbing hold of them, bringing them here only to die or become a monster.

He took one last glance at what he'd just left.

The little girl had crawled from the amauti and was now walking into the terrible ice shards he'd come through. She was looking for the others. She cried out hesitantly. A wail called back in return. The little girl sprinted into the maze of ice, without a glance at the mess that Pitu had created.

Walking away from that little girl haunted him more than anything that had ever happened to him. He felt like a coward for abandoning her, even though the child had told him to leave.

Pitu was in the spirit world. That was about the only thing he knew.

And he was terrified.

10

Demons

Stories he had heard as a child were springing up and whispering into Pitu's memory. The haunting tales of a madman with long nails used to tickle his victims, making them laugh themselves to death. The tales of giants kidnapping people. The stories of ghosts in the distance who led you to your death.

There were good spirits and bad, of course, but there were also tricksters and hunters and all those in between. His encounter with the qallupilluit had made him realize that perhaps many other creatures he had thought to be make-believe were here, too.

Unsure of how to move forward and find safety, Pitu simply walked. His instincts told him to make his way to the mountains that he could see in the distance. He hoped that they might provide safety and cover, perhaps shelter. Whatever else was out here, he wanted to be able to find shelter and protect himself. Mountains also usually meant wildlife: hares, foxes, and maybe even some ptarmigan.

Pitu chose not to think that there might not be any animals at all. That could mean starvation. But he could not ignore that there were hardly any signs of life.

There were no birds in the sky, nor any tracks on the ground. When he dug into the snow to see the ice, he realized it was much too thick to attempt to open a breathing hole. Though he knew that there was always life in the sea, it would take too much energy and time to open the hole, and then wait. All his life, he was taught how to stand at a breathing hole for hours on end until a seal would finally emerge, but that would be too dangerous here. In the wilds of the spirit world, he had no way of knowing what to expect. At least at home, there weren't any powerful creatures with unknown abilities. At home, the creatures were as fallible as he was.

He rested one night in a haphazard iglu. There was a bad taste in his mouth, which held off his hunger for the first night. His thoughts kept returning to the poor children in the qallupilluq's amauti. There were never any stories that addressed what happened to the stolen children, as if they were just legends told to teach caution. Perhaps, over the generations, the truth of the stories was lost, and the myth replaced it. Pitu slept fitfully, nightmares waking him often.

The next day, with little sleep, Pitu continued his trek to the mountains. The rugged rocks reaching into the sky never seemed to grow much larger as he kept walking. For hours he'd go without stopping, keeping pace and walking through the unchanging light of the strange land of spirits. He rested briefly, and not often. When he felt too tired to go on, he'd build another iglu and think of the poor children again, pushing away any hunger pains with ease.

By the third day, the thoughts no longer worked. By the fourth, Pitu could not ignore the screaming in his stomach. The snow he ate quenched his thirst for only short periods of time. He'd started walking that day with dread filling his body. Pitu had no food, and he'd emptied his stomach when he had panicked during the fight with the qallupilluit. His dread was soon replaced by anger. He was lost, his dogs had left him, and he was hungry. To reiterate the last part, his stomach rumbled and growled.

Once the rumbling in his stomach stopped, however, the growling continued.

He stiffened. Pitu had been careless today. He wasn't keeping an eye on his surroundings. Instead, he was thinking too much of home and food and stories. Pitu turned around slightly to see a gigantic black wolf.

Black wolves are almost unheard of this far north, he thought, as he went into slight shock. They lived far away, down where the driftwood grew. Most wolves this far north were grey or white. This wolf growling at him was too large to be an actual wolf; it was the size of a bear. Its eyes were red and menacing. Its teeth were bared in drooling excitement at the prospect of a fresh kill.

Other wolves were approaching from a great distance away. They were dots on the horizon, but even from this far away, Pitu could tell they were smaller than the huge one in front of him, closer to the size of a regular wolf. Pitu did not want to wait for them to arrive. He moved slowly around to face the giant black wolf, and it monitored his movement. Pitu gripped his harpoon firmly, just as he had earlier with the qallupilluq. He inhaled deeply and … the wolf jumped. It landed on top of him before he could throw the harpoon. Pitu fell under the tremendous weight, his arms pinned down. He could feel the wolf's hot breath and saliva on his face. He shouted, but the wolf only snarled and jutted its muzzle out to bite his face.

Pitu pushed against the large wolf and managed to shift its weight enough for him to throw the creature off. He turned onto his stomach to try and get back on his feet, but the wolf was on top of him again in an instant. Pitu put his arms and hands over the back of his head and neck to protect himself, but doing that meant he had to let go of his weapons.

The wolf pounced, thrusting both its paws aggressively in between Pitu's shoulders. The force of each strike pushed the air from Pitu's lungs until there was no time for him to catch his breath. His vision faded. With one last, desperate attempt to free himself, Pitu removed his arms from the protective position and reached out to find his harpoon or knife.

As he reached out, the wolf stopped hitting Pitu's shoulder blades. Instead it began to tear at his parka. He could feel the claws digging into his back, could feel the warmth of his blood flowing from a wound. Finally, his hand brushed over one of his weapons. Pitu was thankful that it was his knife. With one last force of strength, Pitu swiped backward with his outstretched arm and connected with the wolf's front leg.

The wolf cried out and backed away in surprise. Pitu crawled up, found his harpoon as his vision slowly returned, and threw it at the crying creature. With another hit, the wolf stopped its attack and backed out of reach. The other wolves were still in the distance, but they would catch up soon.

Pitu knew that the wolf was not going to die from its wounds. He was conflicted. Should he kill it and run? Should he just leave it and hope to outrun it and the others? Of course, he could not outrun a pack of wolves, especially one with a leader the size of a bear. This decision would have been easy if he were in a normal situation. He would just kill it and leave, making sure he found shelter before the others followed, if they did follow. But in the spirit world, what did it mean to kill a beast such as this? Would it curse him or would it help him?

With little faith in his decision, Pitu ran away.

Pitu had a good head start. Once he looked back, he saw that four other wolves had reached their leader, still tending to its wounds. The wolves held back, not pursuing him quite yet. The creatures were calculative, strategizing a way to attack Pitu, rather than chasing after him. The terror clutched at him as he realized just how intelligent those wolves were. Pitu was more frightened than he had ever been in his life.

Pitu sprinted toward the mountains. There he could protect himself. If only Pitu had his supplies. As it was, he needed to clean the blood off his weapons to ensure that they stayed sharp. He also needed to repair his parka, and his wounds needed to be cleaned and covered.

He had lost too much energy from lack of food and the fight with the wolf to keep going. He needed to rest and drink water. He looked back again. This time the wolves were nowhere to be seen. They would be back, he knew.

With his few options, Pitu built a feeble iglu and hoped it would be shelter enough for the next attack. He had no bowl or lamp to melt snow to make water, so he just ate snow to quench his thirst and distract himself from his aching stomach.

After only a moment of rest, Pitu got his knife and harpoon, cleaned the blood off, and wished—not for the first time—that his dogs hadn't run away. He could have taken oil from the seal fat that fuelled his lamps and spread it on the blade of his knife and on the end of the harpoon. Next he took off his parka and the inner layer of caribou skin he used as a sweater. He saw tears in the backs of the clothing, and decided there was nothing he could do for now. He was relieved, at least, that the rips were not as bad as he thought they would be.

He twisted awkwardly around to see the wounds on his back. The bruises on his shoulders were already turning purple, and there was one deep scratch on his right shoulder blade where the wolf's claw had dug in, but the other scratches were shallow and nothing to worry about. Pitu laid a wad of snow on the deep wound and gritted his teeth against the stinging sensation. He took off his boot, removed the second layer—a sealskin slipper—leaving the first layer of caribou skin sock on his foot. He used his knife to cut the slipper in half. He put one half in his mouth and the other atop his wound to wipe the blood.

Once he put his boot back on, he took off his other boot and did the same thing with the other slipper, but instead of cutting it in half, he cut it open so it could lie flat and large. Taking the caribou skin rope used to tighten his boots around his shins and calves, he tied the two lengths into one long piece. At two ends of his open slipper, Pitu cut little slits and wove the rope through them. He then laid the sealskin slipper onto his shoulder and tied the rope around his chest in a makeshift dressing.

He put his parka, sweater, and boot back on. The boots were loose and would make running more difficult. It was lucky that Pitu's parka was long. He cut the hem into two long and thin strips and tied them around his shins tight enough that they would not come loose if he ran, and loose enough that they did not cut off his circulation.

Pitu sucked on the half of his slipper that was in his mouth. It tasted like old, stale seal and feet. He alternated between eating snow and sucking on the sealskin until he could hear something breathing outside of his iglu.

As quietly as he could, Pitu put the sealskin into

his pocket and got a hold of his weapons. A thunderous howl broke the silence. In the blink of an eye, Pitu's iglu was caved in and a heavy, familiar weight was on top of him again. He saw the red eyes of the black wolf shining in the grey light. The wolf snarled, but the snow protected Pitu slightly from the sharp claws and teeth.

There was no panic stopping and confusing Pitu this time. With all his strength, he thrust his harpoon forward, connecting with the wolf's side again. With his other hand, he swiped upward and connected with the beast's belly. The wolf cried and leaped back. Pitu sat up.

The black wolf ran behind the other wolves.

These were not wolves at all, Pitu realized. They were the size of wolves, they had the large, bushy tails of wolves, they had the teeth and claws, but something made them terrifyingly off-putting. Their eyes were human and their fur was fine and shiny. The sounds they made were like laughing or crying children.

The shock, this time, did not cause Pitu to be useless. He got to his feet and started swiping his harpoon to make them back away. From behind, he could hear a growl. In a flash, he turned around with his knife ready, and one of the wolves caught the knife in a deep slash on its stomach. The creature died.

Howls pierced the night. Pitu swivelled around to see the black wolf standing on all fours and staring at him. The others still circled him, but all his attention was on the black wolf. The two stared at each other, and Pitu knew that the black wolf was saying something to him, but their difference in species and spirituality limited their understanding of each other.

Pitu stretched his arms outward, inviting the next attack.

One of the small wolfish creatures lunged at him. Pitu extended his harpoon and caught the creature in its ribs. Another lunged a second later and he did the same thing with his knife. Three wolves lay around the crumpled iglu, dead.

The howling stopped. The other wolves loped off back in the direction they had come, but Pitu and the black wolf gazed at each other. Each was sizing the other up.

The wolf turned its back on Pitu and caught up with its smaller cousins. Pitu quickly cleaned his weapons and ran in the opposite direction, back on his trek toward the mountains.

11

Giant

*B*y the time Pitu felt sure that the creatures were not going to follow him, he was exhausted. Though he knew he could still be in danger, he could no longer find the strength to build a proper shelter. His adrenaline from the last fight had worn him thin. He began to build an iglu, but the snow was not hard enough to cut blocks. The boy instead dug a shallow hole the length of his body, with a measly wind shelter on one side to protect him slightly from the elements.

Normally, Pitu had trouble falling asleep in shelters of this kind; they were uncomfortable and dangerous. Though they provided slight cover, the soft snow was no protection from animals. Pitu knew that if the wolfish creatures reached him, he'd have no chance of survival. With no energy to fight, he'd be killed in a moment.

Let them kill me, Pitu thought. *I'm never getting out of this place anyway.* With that realization, Pitu fell into a dead sleep. Curled into a ball, he dreamt of the fox and the old man.

The landscape was summery, the tundra covered in moss and lichen. A caribou hide tent was propped in the middle of a gravelly area. The fox was skirting around the edge of the campground. Its coat was a spotty, dirty black colour to blend in with the black lichen–covered rocks, its eyes dark and focused in the direction that Pitu was watching from. There was a small fire directly in front of the tent; a rack made of flat rocks was lying on top of it, holding up a stone bowl full of boiling meat. The old man sat on a boulder the size of one of Pitu's huskies. Thoughts of Miki sprang to Pitu's mind. His stomach twisted with the thought of his dog.

The old man tended to the bowl of *uujuq*, cooking meat, in silence. When Pitu began to walk closer, he looked up and sighed. "You again?" he asked. "Why do I always see you? What do you want?"

"Who are you?" Pitu asked.

"I am Taktuq," the old man answered, spitting out the words. "'Fog,' that is what the spirits call me."

"Why do I keep seeing you?"

"How should I know?" Taktuq said irritably. "Didn't you hear my name? I sit here confused in the clouds all day."

"Taktuq …" Pitu thought of the shaman that Tagaaq had told him about. The shaman had vanished. No one heard from him or saw him ever again. "Taktuq … Are you the shaman that was once revered by all?"

"Revered?" Taktuq growled out a laugh. "Hah! Never. I am the shaman that could never find peace."

Despite his dismissal, Pitu was sure that this was the old shaman he needed to find. He asked, "Where are you? I need you to help me."

"You aren't very smart, are you?" Taktuq replied. "I don't know where I am. I'm LOST."

"How can you be lost?" In his frustration, Pitu began yelling at the old man. He'd moved closer to where Taktuq sat, but felt that if he went any closer he'd be sent back to his mind and awoken from the sleep he so desperately needed. In the distance, now that he thought of his real body, he could hear a thunderous thump that sounded only a short distance away. Pitu focused on the old man again. "You're a shaman. You can't get lost—the spirits are supposed to help you! You can't be lost! You have to help me!"

"The spirits cannot help a soul that is broken, young shaman. That is why you are lost, too."

"Don't talk to me as if you know what is happening," Pitu spat. "You were guided here by your spirit, weren't you? I've been thrown into chaos! You have no idea what it's like in the open land of spirits.

You sit here in your comfortable summer."

"That may be true." Taktuq shrugged. "It's been a long time since I left this place. The air feels too hungry when I step onto the snow." He shivered as the thought of the frozen land made him cold. "I will try to send someone to help you."

Taktuq looked at the fox and whistled lowly. It turned in the opposite direction and dashed away, disappearing from sight much faster than it should have. Pitu heard another thump not too far away; this time he also felt it. He tried to step closer to the summer landscape that was just beyond his reach. The ground beneath his feet splintered as the world around him began to quake. He stopped, spreading his arms wide in hopes that the world would stop quivering under his feet. There was another loud thump, this time only a short distance away. The old man didn't seem to notice.

Suddenly, the fox was back in view. The earth under Pitu's feet quaked again, making him topple onto his back. His eyelids became heavy, and just as he emerged from his dream, he heard the shaman say, "Your guide will find you soon. Don't move from where you are when you wake!"

However, this was easier said than done.

When Pitu opened his eyes and was back in his body, he was looking right into a humongous face. He jumped at the sight of the giant, holding back a high-pitched scream. He calmed himself to hide his fear. He played cool, like a cornered lemming would, until he could think of a plan to get away.

The giant was staring at him in amused curiosity. The eyes were a dark shade of brown, almost black. Greasy shafts of hair hung around the sides of the face; a giant nose was less than an arm's length away from Pitu's own. There was a grinning mouth with only a handful of brownish teeth full of dark black spots around their roots.

And the smell! Pitu tried to hold his breath, but the smell was atrocious. He couldn't remember a worse odour filling his nose. His eyes watered at the stench. Even a thousand caches of igunaq did not smell that awful.

The giant's mouth moved and a high-pitched voice bellowed, "_Kinakuluugavit?_ Who are you?"

Pitu shrieked, trying to squirm away from the giant. It towered over him, laughing at his fright. His attempt at escape was quickly thwarted as the giant grabbed Pitu around his midriff and called out, "You are so TINY!" The giant's laughter filled Pitu's ears, making his eardrums ring. "Who are you, TINY ONE?"

"Who are you?" Pitu shrieked back.

The giant laughed again. "Aaah!" it said. "Ah! You are so cute! Even your voice squeaks like a little lemming!"

Pitu was offended. "I am a great hunter!" he yelled in his deepest voice. "I do NOT sound like a lemming!"

"Oh, little lemming, I will keep you!"

He thrashed against the giant, trying with all his might to squirm free. The struggle was useless. Pitu decided that it would be more frugal of him to save his strength. The giant picked him up and shifted his arms and legs as if checking to see how well they could move. As the giant inspected Pitu, he began to inspect the giant, too.

He couldn't tell whether it was male or female. Though the voice was high and relatively soft—for a giant—it had prominently male features. It was large enough to make a fully grown beluga appear as a seal, a polar bear as a puppy. The clothing was shabby; the upturned caribou hide fading with age and the residue of a thousand messy meals and unkempt days. Pitu wondered how many caribou it had taken to make the parka in the first place. There were stitches all over it.

The giant smiled widely, its breath fuming out of its mouth in stinking wafts. Pitu almost gagged on the smell. The giant spoke in an ancient dialect of Inuktitut, so Pitu struggled to understand all that was coming out of its mouth. To distract himself, he again asked the giant, "Who are you?"

The giant chuckled with pure mirth. "Ah! When you speak it makes me so happy!" The giant stomped its feet in a giddy fashion, then it began to walk away from the little shelter Pitu had made, leaving Pitu's knife and harpoon behind. "I am Inukpak!" the giant said. *Inukpak*, thought Pitu, *a giant named Giant*.

"Tiny Hunter, that is you, and I will keep you to hunt for little things!"

"Inukpak, my tools!" Pitu shrieked. "I cannot be a little hunter without my tools!"

He felt his cheeks flush with embarrassment as he referred to himself as a "little hunter."

Inukpak laughed again, bouncing Pitu around in a disorienting jaunt. The giant continued forward, moving with incredible speed. "Silly little hunter!" Inukpak cooed. "I will make new gear. Ones that are not so sharp. I don't want you to hurt yourself."

"How can I hunt without a harpoon sharp enough to pierce a seal?" Pitu countered. "Or a polar bear?" *Or a giant?* he thought to himself.

"It's okay!" Inukpak still seemed far too cheery for Pitu to truly believe. No one could be that happy. "You're just going to be playing!"

Pitu tried to think of more ways to convince Inukpak that he needed to get his weapons, but he was still tired from the day before and his mind was slow. He couldn't come up with a plan that would leave him in one piece. He knew that if he could just get out of Inukpak's grip, he could run back to his makeshift shelter and retrieve his tools and find a way to outrun the giant.

Pitu looked over his shoulder and was

disheartened to see that his shelter was no longer anywhere in sight. They had gone much farther, with much greater speed, than Pitu had ever thought possible. Suddenly, he grew incredibly tired, without any energy to become angry. With careless abandon, he let Inukpak take him deeper into the land of spirits than he could ever truly begin to understand. *I am never leaving this place,* he thought. *I will never go back home to see my family again.*

By the time the giant stopped walking, Pitu had lost feeling in his lower body. He looked up into the sky to try to gauge the time, but it remained an unshifting overcast grey, revealing nothing. However, he knew they had been travelling for a long period of time because his body ached as though he'd been on a day-long qamutiik ride. They were near the distant mountains that Pitu had been trying to reach since he arrived. With the large steps that Inukpak took, it dawned on Pitu just how long it would have taken him to journey that far with just his two feet. The trip had taken Inukpak hours, yet the giant was still jaunty and annoyingly cheerful.

Inukpak climbed through passages in the mountains with ease, following a path that no human could see simply because of the great distances cleared by each step. Pitu thought of the glaciers back home, how they seemed to crush mountains with their weight and the endless stream of melting waters that slid down to the ocean in summer, following a path that was large and wide. Did giants create those paths in the past? Were giants somehow responsible for the glaciers that brought so much life to his world? Pitu shook his head, the thoughts jumbling his mind.

They came to a full stop in a valley surrounded by a bowl of mountains. There was no iglu, but there were plenty of other things that would make living here comfortable. *Do giants feel the cold?* Pitu thought. This one didn't seem to.

In the valley, there was a herd of caribou that made Pitu's mouth water. There were other animals, too. Their arrival woke a polar bear from a doze; wolves (that were, thankfully, normal wolves) wagged their tails in greeting. They all swarmed around Inukpak, little pets greeting their master. The sight perplexed Pitu.

The giant put a hand into the pocket of its parka, bringing out a giant handful of other animals. The giant dropped the lemmings, hares, and foxes into the middle of the wolves, and then took out a seal for the polar bear to eat on its own. Pitu's stomach grumbled as he watched.

"Oh, little hunter," Inukpak said. "Are you hungry, too?"

"Yes," Pitu grudgingly replied.

"You can have a caribou!" Inukpak said. "What do you want? The ribs? The leg? The head?"

Pitu perked up at that. The head was the best part of the caribou, with its brains, eyeballs, and most of all, its tongue and jaw. Inukpak laughed again. "The head it is, little hunter!"

12

Stolen

Pitu was in Inukpak's camp for days, and his dreams had suddenly stopped. He slept in Inukpak's sleeve, since the giant did not have a knife or any tools small enough for Pitu to use to build an iglu or construct a small tent. He missed his harpoon and knife, often finding himself wondering what had happened to them.

Pitu missed a lot of things. His mother, mostly, but his dogs, too. His sewing kit, his tools, his life. He thought of Saima all the time, thinking of how hurt she must be. Had his dogs returned to camp? Had she seen them, and was she thinking he was dead? How would his mother cope with the thought? Were the hunters out searching for him?

Now that he had been gone for more than a week, Pitu was growing restless and angry. He wanted to go home. He wanted to fight the wolves and any other creature he might encounter. He wanted to find the shaman and force him to bring him back to the world of the living. The little bit of peace Pitu had found within himself last summer had faded, leaving behind only a feeling of bitterness.

There was nothing to do at the giant's camp, though. The valley was huge and Pitu was simply a little speck in the middle of it. The herd of caribou was unafraid of Pitu, so he often found himself weaving through them to feel better. They were such calm and docile creatures that when he would pet their thick-furred bodies, his anger thinned out, absorbed by the softness of their coats.

The other animals were tame, too. The polar bear, especially. The wolves were not too different from Pitu's own dog team, and perhaps for that reason he often thought of his team back home. The polar bear was ridiculous, jumping and doing tricks for the giant. It was unlike anything he'd ever seen. The bear would roll onto its back so the giant would rub its belly, or it would sit and shake its paw so that Inukpak would give it a fish as a treat.

Maybe, if he ever returned home, Pitu would try to teach Miki these tricks. He shook his head. What a silly thought.

Inukpak did not eat often, and never seemed to need to relieve himself. Or herself. To be honest, Pitu still could not tell whether Inukpak was male or female, and he didn't plan on asking the giant. Inukpak appeared to be male, but the giant's mannerisms were distinctly female. Not wanting to think too much and become confused, Pitu decided not to label Inukpak. Whatever the giant was, it wasn't Pitu's business, because the giant acted like a child anyway.

"Little hunter!" Inukpak shouted. Pitu's ears rang, since the only way the giant communicated was with loud and joyful shouts. "Little hunter!"

Pitu emerged from the caribou herd. "What?"

"Oh, there you are!" Inukpak laughed an annoyingly high-pitched laugh. "I lost you! I have to go and get food for my pets. Make sure the animals do not run away!"

Without another word or glance, Inukpak left the valley. In four strides, the giant cleared the mountains and Pitu was alone with a playful polar bear, tame wolves, and a herd of caribou. Thoughts of escape instantly sprang to mind. He could run away, try to find the guide that Taktuq had sent for him ... but then he remembered, he'd have no weapons to use to protect himself from the creatures he would definitely encounter.

He thought about riding on the back of a caribou, but that was a ridiculous thought. The caribou wouldn't know what to do and he wouldn't either.

What if he brought the wolves with him? They would protect him from the evil creatures that lived in this world. That, too, was not a good idea. No matter how tame these wolves may have seemed, they were still wild creatures. They also had a great fondness for Inukpak, much like Pitu's dogs had for him back home …

The bear was out of the question. Pitu had been too afraid of the animal to even go near it.

Pitu's shoulder had grown sore and he was sure the wound was inflamed. It pounded with heated pain. He hadn't looked at it since wrapping it up, and he hadn't changed the covering either. He could run away, and maybe he'd be found by Taktuq's guide. The trouble with that option was that even though he was now well fed, and he would be able to bring some caribou meat for the trip, the wound on his back made him weak. He would grow tired too quickly for it to make a difference in his departure. Pitu might not even make it out of the valley.

As he plotted to make an escape, he neglected his surroundings. Again.

At various intervals in the valley, dark shapes emerged and stalked toward the giant's camp. The caribou became skittish; the wolves howled and barked. Pitu didn't notice their changing behaviour until the polar bear moved next to him, stood on its hind legs, and roared.

Sure that the polar bear was about to attack him, Pitu jumped to his feet. The bear went back down on his front legs and gestured its nose around the valley. Pitu followed the movement, landing his eyes on the familiar hulking figure of the black wolf with red eyes.

This is it, Pitu thought, *I'm dead. The wolves have found me and I have nothing to defend myself with. I'm dead.*

And it seemed as though he was right. The

dark wolves all surged forward, closing around him in a wide circle. There were more of them now than when he had encountered them last time. These ones were all black, although none of the others shared the leader's glowing red eyes. These ones also did not have the creepy human characteristics. They, thankfully, did not sound like laughing children. These were pure and vicious black wolves. Pitu had an inkling that these wolves were tougher than the ones he had encountered before.

The leader strode forward toward Pitu, and the others growled and frightened the caribou and Inukpak's wolves. The leader tried to retrieve Pitu, but the polar bear attacked. The bear stood on its hind legs again and roared. The wolf paid it little attention. Instead it sprinted forward in a flash and slashed its claws across the bear's chest.

This didn't faze the bear as it came down to its front legs and quickly darted forward, locking its jaws on the wolf's neck. Since the wolf and the bear were basically the same size, the wolf wriggled out of the bear's grasp easily and dragged its claws over the bear's face, cutting deep gashes into its muzzle and nearly wounding its eyes.

It became clear that the bear would not stop fighting. The other wolves pounced, locking their jaws onto the bear's legs and slashing huge cuts into the bear's sides. With the bear distracted, the lead wolf leaped toward a flabbergasted Pitu, and clamped its teeth onto one of his legs.

The wolf dragged Pitu away, and the other wolves, no longer needing to fight the bear, ran to protect the leader. They loped off at an amazing speed, leaving Inukpak's valley and animals behind.

13

Rescue

Pitu struggled against the wolf's grip, attempted to kick the beast and hit it with his fists. When that failed, he twisted and writhed. When that also failed, he reached out, trying to grab hold of the creature's fur or limbs. The pain grew unbearable. He could feel himself getting closer to blacking out. All the motion caused the wolf to slow and let go of his leg, and he felt instantly relieved. As he lay on the ground, the other wolves stepped on Pitu's limbs to prevent him from fighting or running.

The wolf then took hold of Pitu's leg and continued running, dragging the hunter behind it. After struggling until there was no strength left in his body, Pitu fell unconscious.

He did not know how much time had passed when he awoke. He was shivering, lying on a soft surface surrounded by sleeping bodies. From all around, he could hear breathing creatures, see their dark shadows. It almost reminded him of being at home in the iglu with his family. He kept his eyes closed for a moment and almost believed that it had all been a dream. The pain soon returned to remind him of all the things that had gone wrong. He thought it all over in his mind:

First, there was that blizzard that made his dogs run away.

Second, that very same blizzard also sent him to the spirit world somehow.

Third, his encounter with the qallupilluit. He'd had to kill one in order to be safe, and he saw a dead child and witnessed a little girl transforming into the very same creature he had just killed.

Fourth, he was attacked by evil, wolfish creatures. Twice.

Fifth, he saw a glimmer of hope when he finally spoke to the old man he saw in his dreams.

Sixth, that glimmer of hope was completely destroyed as a giant came and abducted him for several days, not to mention losing his weapons in the process.

And finally, now, he had been attacked and taken hostage by the dark wolves. There was also his mangled leg and wounded shoulder to consider.

Pitu saw the sleeping wolves all around him. They were various shapes and sizes, and they all looked a lot less evil while they slept. Then again, Pitu thought the same thing of Atiq and his unending energy when he slept, too. The body of the leader was right at Pitu's feet. The wolf seemed small now, almost normal. Its black fur was darker than the night sky, like it was covered in the soot from a qulliq. The other wolves were dark, too, but a shade that did not suggest pure malice.

The large wolf shifted its weight, making Pitu glance over. He could see that the creature's red eyes were alert, staring intently at its prey. The wolf really was terrifying. In only a moment, the rest of the wolves opened their eyes and gazed at him, too. The yellow glares were uncanny, eerie, as if they had a thousand ghost stories behind each blink. Pitu shuddered.

All the wolves stood, stretched, and waited.

The leader took its time before it looked back at Pitu. It yawned and stretched like the others, limbering up its muscles. *Is this it?* Pitu mused. *Is this when I die?*

The wolf, though, just leaned down and sunk its sharp teeth into his leg. Pitu cried out, the pain reverberating throughout his whole body, from his brain to his armpits to his fingers and toes. He arched his back against the pain, but that only twisted his leg in the wolf's mouth, creating more agony. The throb had been dull when he was lying down, but now it sang like a raven. Pain squawked from his leg and outward with every step the wolf took, dragging Pitu along.

At some point, the echoes of a distant scream reached their ears, and Pitu thought he recognized it as the voice of Inukpak as the giant reached its camp and discovered the injured bear and the little hunter missing. At least that's what he dreamt: the giant, in a vengeful rage, following the tracks of the wolves and chasing them in an attempt to rescue the lost little hunter.

Pitu later realized that it had been his own voice he heard.

The wolves ran without slowing down or stopping. Pitu drifted in and out of consciousness, often hallucinating between each time he closed and opened his eyes. In confusion, he saw images of his family filled with grief, of the fox he called Tiri in a fit of frustration, of the faces of those in the village he lived in. His whole body ached with the infection that was doubtlessly swimming in his blood. The smooth surface of the ground made the trip as minimally comfortable as being dragged alongside a vicious pack of depraved dark wolves could be.

Pitu often woke up in the same manner as before, in the middle of a circle, the wolves taking a small rest. They usually woke up at the same time he did or right after, and continued the tireless running. Pitu did not know the destination or what they were running to, and he did not want to find out. *Perhaps these wolves of the spirit world don't eat, and they throw their prey off cliffs?* Pitu thought. *Perhaps they have a sacred spot for killing and eating their capture?* Whatever it was, Pitu imagined a million ways to die, often by the very fangs that were sunk into his leg.

He dreamt of Taktuq or the fox occasionally, but only in short bursts. He never saw any sign of a guide searching for him. Granted, he was often unconscious. Pitu had no idea how long the wolves had been running, but it felt like a year of this endless cycle of waking and fading, waking and fading, waking and fading.

Once, he awoke to the same circle, surrounded by the same wolves with the same sounds he always awoke to. With his little strength, Pitu sat up shakily to get a look at his leg. The pathetic thing was mottled black, with various puncture wounds where the wolf's teeth had locked onto it over and over again. He cried at the sight, having been unaware that it had gotten that bad. The pain continued to bother him, but at that point, he'd been feeling it for so long that the agony was now disconnected from him, only coming back in short bursts from time to time.

Pitu screamed an anger-filled bawl. He had grown hopeless and weak and he missed his mother. He missed Saima. He missed Natsivaq and Atiq and Arnaapik and Anaana and Saima and all of them all over again. He wondered if he would ever get to marry Saima, the girl that always made him laugh with admiration and nervousness. He wondered if he would ever get to hold Natsivaq's children—his little sisters and brothers—again. He wondered if he would ever wake up to see Anaana tending to the qulliq. If they would ever share a silly story with each other in the quiet mornings when Arnaapik and Atiq were still sound asleep. Would he ever scold Atiq again for his restlessness? Would he ever praise Arnaapik for her maturity and skills as a seamstress? He sobbed louder. Would he ever survive?

The wolves woke and stood, stretched, completed their regular waking-up routine. They stared at Pitu, as he was crying. He clutched helplessly at his dying leg, banged his mitted hands against the soft snow on the ground. The leader looked at his wolves, and gestured that they were to pick up the young hunter once more.

Each wolf took a limb and moved the boy at a leisurely pace. Pitu still wailed in an endless screech, his sobs wracking through his ribs and outward into the sky, as if he were calling for help. Except now he cried for reasons much greater than the pain of the wolves' bites. He cried because the unknown was terrifying to him. He didn't know if he would ever see those he loved again, or find Taktuq to teach him the wisdom of shamans. He had no idea where the wolves were taking him and he didn't know if he had any strength left in him to survive another night among the vicious creatures of the spirit world. The young hunter was dying.

I am dying, Pitu thought with unbreakable clarity. Perhaps this is what Tagaaq and his mother meant when they spoke of the darkness they sensed inside of him. His hysterics began to lessen now as he thought of the inevitability of his death. The end of his life was near, he could taste it like bile at the back of his throat. It wasn't calm that was overtaking him, however—it was a sense of heaviness, the thickening of the blood in his veins making him lethargic, unable to fight.

Once his sobs finally quieted, he felt numb. The wolves holding his limbs began to jog, carrying him stretched in a spread-eagle posture. He went limp, forgetting the pain and forgetting to struggle to stay alive.

Pitu was not proud of his lament. He was embarrassed and upset, but he was drained, unable to control his emotions. There were no other hunters around to judge him, no other humans who could tell the story of a young hunter crying remorselessly, gripped by the teeth of half a dozen wolves.

He even began to miss the company of Inukpak.

The crying had released a feeling of resolve that slowly bloomed within him. He was dying, the infection in his wounds made that evident. There were no herbs or remedies that could heal a leg that had turned black. Maybe he could be saved by cutting it off, but there was no way he could do it without help from another person.

I will not see my family again, he told himself. *But I will join my father soon.*

It was then, when he thought of his father, that he gained a blinding strength. Pitu felt it ripple through his body, making him feel, for the first time, that he had more power than the black wolves. A memory sprang to his mind, people of his village calling him a name he was embarrassed by, but now it was the only thing that gave him strength. He fought against the grip of each wolf's jaws, shook himself loose from their grasp and stood, putting little weight on his right leg. He ignored the pain, ignored that his vision was blurry.

"I am Piturniq the Great Hunter," he screamed at the wolves, his voice hoarse from the crying. "I will not die like a coward."

The giant black wolf growled with rage. The wolves all seemed alarmed by this.

Pitu was shocked by his surge of energy, too. He felt the adrenaline rushing from his skin again in a confused frenzy, painting his vision with ugly pink-and-yellow stars. He sagged and fell over.

He woke again some time later, face down in the snow, but alone. There was no enclosure of black bodies surrounding him, no calm breath of sleeping wolves. His aching body throbbed feverishly, even though he could see there was a cold wind blowing snow. With all his strength, Pitu slowly rolled over and pushed himself to stand again.

In one direction, he could see nothing but a barren expanse of land with snow-covered hills, and in the distance, Inukpak's mountains gleaming. In the other direction, he could see the sun on the horizon, shining bright like midsummer.

The light registered slowly in his mind. In a daze, he began to limp toward it, thinking no doubt that this was the path to death and all the luxuries death would bring. No hunger, no pain, no memory.

He stumbled. Crawled toward his death. He fell unconscious. Woke. Crawled. *Why can't I just die right here and right now?* he questioned the spirits. *Why do I have to work so hard to reach the end?*

But, after what felt like years, after each gruelling use of strength to crawl along the ground toward the edge of his life, he could finally see past the sunlight.

He saw the fox, standing with its nose in the air, staring at him.

"Help," Pitu cried, though he was unsure if he actually spoke or if he simply thought it.

14

The Shaman

Pitu woke up to the pattern of a dried skin tent above and supple, warm caribou furs enveloping him. Soft sunlight shone through little holes in the skin of the tent, making him squint as he looked around. He sighed, felt pain in his sides, but also a sense of safety. There was no strength left in his body, only the feeble feeling that he wasn't dead. Everything around him was silent, except for the distinct crackling of a hot fire outside the tent.

Though he had no strength, he managed a little movement, jostling a creature he didn't know was sleeping against his side. It was the fox he called Tiri. Pitu looked at the creature now, seeing its transparent iridescence. The fox glowed faintly, colours fading in and out of its fur. Pitu blinked hard and gazed at the fox again, seeing that it was more than just a mortal creature.

"What are you?" Pitu said, thinking out loud.

"Alone for decades, and the first shaman that finds me," said a cranky voice, "doesn't even recognize his own *tuurngaq*. Hah!"

Through the entrance of the tent, with his neck barely able to lift his head far enough to see, Pitu's eyes met with those of a wise old elder. He had white rings around his eyes like Tagaaq, but that is where their similarities stopped. This old man held no calmness in him, no peace or serenity. There was a storm across his face, unfaltering bursts of distaste and irritability clouding his wisdom.

"Tuurngaq?" Pitu asked.

"You don't know what a tuurngaq is?" The old man shook his head. "You told me you were a shaman! What kind of a shaman are you, if you don't even know what a tuurngaq is?"

"I never said I'm a shaman."

"Well, the fox told me," the elder said.

"Am I dead?" Pitu asked, wanting to change the subject.

"You wish!" the old man said. "You're in the land of the dead, pretty much. It's rather unpleasant, isn't it? You almost died! Your tuurngaq made me save you. Rotten luck."

"What do you mean?"

"What do I mean? What do I mean?" The old man shook his head again. "What do I mean! I mean you can't ever leave this horrible place. No, no, no. You come here because you are not welcome in the land of the living and then you can't ever redeem yourself so you live alone with you—"

The old man stopped talking, shook his head again. The storm continued to rage across his face. Pitu was stuck underneath the covers of the bedding. Rather abruptly, he realized that he was completely naked. He hoped that his clothes weren't too far away, but for now, he soaked in the comfort of the caribou skins.

"In the land of the living, we hunt to stay alive," the old man said finally. "In the land of the dead, there's nothing for the living to hunt."

Confused, Pitu remarked, "I thought you said you had been here for decades."

"So?"

"So, how did you live here for so long if there's nothing to hunt?"

"There is nothing to hunt!"

"So, how did you survive?"

The old man shook his head. "You ask too many questions."

Pitu wanted to point out that he'd only asked the same question in three different ways. He chose not to respond, soon falling back into unconsciousness.

He woke later to the old man spitting something

mushy from his mouth to his hand and putting it on Pitu's leg. The limb had gone numb. Dazedly, Pitu said, "My leg is too far gone—it died before I did. You have to cut it off."

"What, you think I can't fix a black leg?" the old man replied. "I can fix a black leg, you ungrateful boy."

Pitu replied by falling back to sleep.

This time he dreamt, not of the fox or the old man, but of his mother. She was tending the qulliq, humming a sad song while the children slept. Pitu sat up in bed and crawled over to her, but he couldn't speak. She sang a sad song for her lost son.

> *My son has gone where the wind only knows* aijaijaa
> *I hear him in my dreams aijaijaa*
> *But dark is his soul aijaijaa*
> *He promised me he would not leave aijaijaa*
> *But his promise has broken aijaijaa*
> *Since he is no longer my son aijaijaa*
> *Oh, Husband, what have you done aijaijaa*
> *You took my boy when he was too young* aijaijaa
> *My son has gone where the wind only knows* aijaijaa
> *When he returns he will be a dark soul aijaijaa*

The song broke Pitu's heart. *Anaana*, he tried to say. *Anaana, I'm coming back.*

⊷⊶⊷

He woke to the old man shaking him. The old man looked grumpy, as he did every other time Pitu had seen and spoken to him.

"You've been sleeping for days," he said, sounding tired. "Eat. I want my bed back."

The old man did not wait. He stuck a spoonful of hot broth into Pitu's mouth. It burned the roof of his mouth, but it tasted good. He did not flinch from the scalding liquid, inhaling the soup. It tasted like boiled seal, with meat cut up into bite-size chunks. The old man fed him without waiting, without letting Pitu savour each bite, and took the bowl away too soon.

Pitu said, "I'm still hungry."

"Good for you, ungrateful boy," was the elder's curt reply.

"Your name was Taktuq, right?" Pitu asked. "Why are you so grumpy?"

The old man shook his head, making Pitu think that it was the old man's habit to shake his head in response to anything. "No manners, ungrateful boy. Didn't your mother ever teach you to respect your elders?"

"Of course she did," Pitu replied. "But I learned to respect elders for their understanding and knowledge and strength and patience. You haven't shown me any of that, so it is quite difficult to respect you without you showing me your wisdom."

"Why would it be hard to respect someone, especially an elder? When I was your age, I respected every person I ever met, ever."

"I see that has changed," Pitu said. "All you do is yell in a cranky voice, calling me an ungrateful boy and telling me I know nothing, when you haven't done anything to teach me."

The old man ignored Pitu's words, and instead laughed. "Hah!"

Pitu did not reply in frustration, as he wanted to. An inkling of his upbringing remained instilled in his mind. He had learned to always respect those who were older than he was, so he ignored his retaliatory self, bit back his response of annoyance.

He felt his stomach grumble in a distressing urge. Pitu sat up immediately. He needed to get out of the tent. His insides were about to burst as he desperately needed to relieve himself. Right that very second. Absolutely immediately.

He threw off the blanket, unabashed by his nakedness. Pitu was amazed to find his leg was only bruised purple. There were disgusting patches of green mush set on the deep punctures from the wolf's teeth that were healing the wounds, but the leg was not black anymore. He moved his arm around and felt that the pain in his shoulder was also gone.

"Told you I can fix a black leg, ungrateful boy."

Pitu stood and ran from the tent, unable to spare time to thank the old man. He was relieved to find that his leg could carry his weight, though barely. His bare feet hurt against the gravel, and he limped badly, but he could walk. He went behind a large boulder and did what his body urgently needed to do.

Quite some time later, he emerged from behind the boulder and limped back toward the tent. The old man was eating a bowl of broth, sitting by the fire. Taktuq did not seem to care that Pitu was naked. Neither of them did.

The camp was on a small island bathed in glowing sunlight. The air was warm, too warm for snow to stick. Yet, on the shoreline, where the ocean met the beach, it was solid ice. Taktuq's tent and fire were on a patch of gravel not too far from the beach, but the rest of the island was covered in soft moss, moistened by a stream and pond in the centre of the island. From the look of it, Pitu figured he could walk around the whole island in less than an hour. It was a lovely place, with the sun shining endlessly, and flowers and berries grew abundantly all the time, but the thought of living here for decades made Pitu feel as if he were in an enclosed space. There was no way that animals lived anywhere on the island, no way that living off the roots and berries and flowers was viable. How did Taktuq survive?

"I figured you would need to do that. You have been asleep for four days. Maybe five," the old man said. "What is your name, anyway?"

"Piturniq," he replied.

"Piturniq," the old man laughed, "Hah! So, what we have here is the most extreme tides, Piturniq, and the fog, Taktuq."

"Why is that funny?"

"It's not!" the old man said. "It's stupid! I am lost and you are crazy."

"I am not crazy," Pitu replied, annoyed.

"Oh, okay, 'Piturniq,'" Taktuq said. "You do realize that the meaning of your name is also when the moon makes people act oddly? Makes them act crazy? You must encompass that quality."

"Extreme tides and the moon are not the same thing."

"Oh, but they are," Taktuq replied.

Hah! Pitu mimicked Taktuq's usual sarcastic laugh in his mind.

Pitu left him then, going back into the tent to find his clothes. He came out and looked around for bones to make a new knife, going to the edge of the beach and rummaging through the pebbles and rocks in search of anything to make tools out of. He found nothing but stones.

He gave up a little while later, his leg growing tired and beginning to throb. As he made his way back toward the camp, Pitu noticed something familiar set down next to the pit of fire Taktuq sat beside. He rushed toward the shapes, finding the knife and harpoon he had left behind when Inukpak took him.

"How did you get these?" Pitu asked as he picked them up. The tools were clean and pristine. In fact, they were in the best condition Pitu had ever seen them.

"The guide I sent for you retrieved them." Taktuq answered the question, surprisingly without lashing out at Pitu.

"Where is this guide?" Pitu was curious, sitting on the ground across the fire, admiring his tools. "I never saw anyone. Only a giant and the dark wolves."

Taktuq did not seem surprised. He continued to converse with Pitu with an air of ease, not bursting with anger as he usually was. "Inukpak is the last giant. She does become very lonely."

"Inukpak was the guide?"

"No!" Taktuq growled. *Oh, there he is*, Pitu thought. "Ungrateful boy! You understand nothing."

Pitu did not reply. Usually, with an elder, Pitu could always keep his composure. He knew to be respectful and to wait until their thoughts were finished. It was difficult with Taktuq, who was a strange old man, never finishing any story and always reacting in a bitter angriness. The old man's face swam in its angry storm, his wrinkles tightening and stretching as he blustered through his words.

"Will you teach me to be a shaman?" Pitu asked, deciding it was time to change the subject.

"No," Taktuq replied. He looked down at his

feet, saddened by the inquiry, not angry or upset. The old man became quiet, murmuring, "There is no good in shamanism."

Pitu wanted to ask why, but he didn't want to suffer another one of Taktuq's outbursts, so he waited in silence. The old man stayed quiet, reliving some past memory that no one really knew except for him. Pitu wondered how this could be the man in Tagaaq's story: the shaman who could build an enormous iglu out of ice, who could fly like a bird in the sky, who could transform into animals in times of distress.

Taktuq tossed a little package to Pitu. It was a tiny bag, similar to one he had in his pack on his qamutiik. He opened it to see an ivory sewing needle and thread made from sinew. Pitu looked back at Taktuq with a question on his face.

"I have some extra skins," Taktuq explained. "You can build yourself a tent."

Pitu wasn't the best at sewing. He was good at minor repairs when on long hunting trips, but to sew his own tent was a daunting task. Taktuq brought some skins out from inside the tent. "Where did you get these?" Pitu asked.

Taktuq sighed at the question, but did not raise his voice in anger. "The spirits offer me animals to make my life more comfortable here when I grow weary of it, but I have lost use for the skins over the years. Now I am going to sleep in my bed." And with that, the old man left.

Pitu did not know a pattern for a tent. Tiri came out of Taktuq's tent and sat next to Pitu. Even though he had been seeing the tuurngaq in his dreams for almost a year, he could not feel at ease with the ethereal creature. At first he felt he could not get used to it, but as they sat together in the calm summer air, they opened up to each other. Tiri did not speak in words, but Pitu understood her as well as he understood himself. They both had little fondness for the old man.

"So, you're a tuurngaq, ai?" Pitu said out loud. "What is a tuurngaq anyway?"

The fox made no sound, yet Pitu heard an answer through the air, unspoken, but true. *We guide shamans and communicate with other spirits on behalf of shamans, mostly. But we can also be companions.*

"So … can you guide me in how to sew a tent together?" Pitu jokingly asked.

Alas, Tiri spoke, *I have no knowledge of this. I do not have thumbs as you do.*

Pitu nodded in understanding. Tiri urged him to continue talking, to tell her stories as he tried to sew the sealskins together into some shape he thought might be tent-ish. There wasn't much on his mind except for his family. He spoke to the ethereal fox the same way Tagaaq used to tell him stories and lessons.

"I miss home. My mother is very good at sewing. She made my tent and my brother's tent. She teaches a lot of the girls in our village, too, if their mothers are too busy. Women do a lot of work. My mother is lucky because she has only two young children now … I know I always say she's old and frail, but she's not too old. She still has many years. Since my father died she has aged a lot, though …

"My father was a good man. He was wise and brave. He was much older than my mother. I miss him a lot. He taught me everything I know about hunting, but he always talked about me like I was not going to live very long. He would say things like, 'He'll need to see this before everything changes,' or 'He won't be this boy forever,' or something like that. I never understood him, but I suppose I kind of do now… He must have known that I was a shaman. I just wish he had told me that before he died.

"I used to dream about Saimaniq a lot before I started dreaming about you, Tiri. She's really beautiful, but that is not why I like her. She's very funny, and she's not very shy. A lot of girls in our village are shy around me because I have always been a good hunter, and parents always tease, saying, 'All the girls will fight over Piturniq.' Or they tell them that if they want to have a good husband, they have to marry someone like me. What a strange thing to hear as you grow up. But Saima never got shy, she always said, 'I won't need to fight for Piturniq—I already have him wrapped around my finger,' and it was true. It was because of her that I remained humble. If I ever returned from a hunt and I was showing off, she would tell me she did not like that, because it is very selfish. If she thinks I've died, will she get married to another man? I wanted her to wait for me, but I don't want her to live her life waiting for me."

Pitu began to cry then. He told Tiri about everyone: Natsivaq, Puukuluk, Atiq and Arnaapik, and Tagaaq. As he sewed his tent, his tears seeped into the skins, making it a part of him. He sewed and told stories until he fell asleep in an upright position next to the burning fire.

15

Shame

"**I**s sleeping the only thing you are good at?" Taktuq asked the next morning as he put a spoonful of broth into a bowl. Pitu yawned and refused to answer. Taktuq had awoken him only a moment before, and his neck and back ached from the awkward sitting position he had stayed in as he slept all night. "Sleeping and crying?"

Pitu wiped his face, knowing that there must have been dried white lines where his tears had streaked down. Pitu didn't want to answer that question either.

Taktuq didn't offer any food to Pitu, instead only feeding himself and putting the empty bowl on the ground when he'd finished eating. Pitu pointed at the bowl and asked, "May I?"

"What am I? Your mother?" Taktuq said hysterically. "Do what you have to do. I'm not going to take care of you!"

Pitu shouldn't have said anything, as he knew that it would be disrespectful to talk back to an elder, but the words "I was just trying to be polite," accidentally slipped out under his breath.

At first, it seemed that the old man did not notice the slip of Pitu's tongue. He shook his head as he always did, right and left and right and left, back and forth. Taktuq stayed silent for a long moment. Pitu took the bowl and put a large spoonful of broth into it, and began to sip at the hot liquid.

It was just as the bowl was against his mouth that Taktuq finally reacted with an angry outburst. "I didn't ask for you to join me here, ungrateful boy!" He was spitting with each word, forcing them out like thunder from the sky above. "You show up here and expect me to care for you? I fixed your leg! Now, go! Go and let the land of the dead kill you like it is meant to."

The outburst had been so sudden that Pitu had dropped the bowl and the scalding liquid fell into his lap. It splashed all over him, burning his legs and hands and little spots on his chin. The old man didn't stop yelling.

"I didn't send for help! I don't need help. I'm not stuck here." Taktuq's voice shook, the storm on his face turning into a black rainfall of rage. "You come and insult me in my home, you disturb the little peace I have. I found this place on my own, you know? I live here alone on purpose. You can't save me, boy. You can't."

Pitu had known the old man was ill tempered and became upset easily. He didn't blame him for the anger, after the tragedy of his family. He understood why the old man was unstable and how he had become like a cloud of rain, gloomy and furious and sad all in one. Taktuq continued to yell at the height his lungs would allow, nasty things that should never be said to another person, things that should not even be thought by a man who often commented about how disrespectful he felt Pitu was. Then Taktuq shut it all off, sat back down, and breathed heavily.

The next words were also an accident, but Pitu didn't try to hide them. Once he started speaking, he didn't stutter to a halt or mutter quietly to himself. "How funny it is for you to tell me to go and let myself die in the land of the dead, when you have been here for decades and you refuse to let it do the same to you," he mused, his voice growing confident. "But it's not so funny because you think you are dead. You are a lonely man with a dead family and you live here in your grief and you refuse to die because you feel like you are dead already. And you feel as though you deserve it."

"You know nothing," Taktuq snarled.

"I don't know anything about you, this is true," Pitu said. "Except for the story that the son of Angugaattiaq the Blind told to me. The story of how your family died and you vanished, and no one saw or heard from you again and no one knew what had happened. I see now that you exiled yourself in your mourning and guilt. I see that you are not lost in the land of spirits because of the environment or because you have just lost the path or direction you came from, but because you have lost your soul."

Taktuq stood up and smacked Pitu's face. "Leave. Now."

Pitu stood up, towering over the old man. "I can't leave a lost man. That would be pitiful."

"Do not pity me." He shook his head. "I don't need any pity. I need you to LEAVE."

The old man pushed at Pitu, but he was weak. Pitu didn't budge, and waited patiently as the man punched him. He was reminded of Atiq's temper tantrums.

"Leave!" the old man shrieked.

"Taktuq," Pitu said, "once known as the greatest shaman of all time. Now sits in the sunlight in constant cowardice. What kind of a person are you? Unable to hunt in the spirit world, yet you live in this comfortable place where the sun never sets and the weather never changes. You have a bowl of broth always cooking and spirits who take care of you. It's despicable. Your village starved in the darkness of your cowardice. You killed people who worshipped you because you were here soaking in your self-pity."

The old man stumbled back, clicking his tongue against the back of his teeth. "Fancy talk for a boy who finds himself in the same place."

"I am no coward," Pitu said, taking a stride forward. "I came here to find you. The winds took me here in a blizzard. I dreamt of this summer island for months because the spirits were telling me I had to find you. I am the next leader of Angugaattiaq's camp, and her spirit tells mine and the others that you need to end your self-pity."

The old man waved a hand in dismissal, shook his head as usual. "Angugaattiaq was a wise woman. She wouldn't send a stupid boy like you on such an errand. She sent you here because you are a nuisance to your camp, a boy of no essence."

Pitu actually laughed, crouching slightly.

Taktuq did not appreciate the laughter. He struck the back of Pitu's head with force.

"You are lost," Pitu said through another laugh, unfazed by Taktuq's strike. "The spirits keep you alive, but they hide from you. Your powers have broken."

"I know that!" Taktuq shouted. "Of course I know that! Why do you think I have them no more? Because I broke them! I broke them myself."

This shocked Pitu, making him lean back a little and focus more on the heaviness in Taktuq's shoulders. Pitu stopped his laughter immediately, choosing instead to approach the topic with a calmer tone. He prompted Taktuq to continue telling his story, curious to find out what had happened to him. "Why would you do such a thing, old man?"

Taktuq clicked his tongue again. "You have no sense of respect."

"I do not respect cowards who let dozens of people parish," Pitu said without hesitation, but his tone remained soft. "Not if that person refuses to move on."

"You know nothing, young man," Taktuq repeated.

"Perhaps I do not."

"You want to know what happened to me?" Taktuq finally said. He sagged down to the rock he always sat upon, defeated. "I will tell you my story."

Pitu sat back down and filled the bowl of broth, eating as he waited for Taktuq to speak. Taktuq shook his head, as if appalled at how comfortable Pitu was even after their screaming argument.

"When I was a young boy," Taktuq began, "I saved a man from drowning in the sea. I had seen him from the beach. He was yelling for help, but no one could hear him except for me. I was all alone, because the other kids didn't like to play with me. They were unnerved by me, I think.

"I was the only one who could see the man, so I took a qajaq from the beach and paddled my way to him with great speed. The man's head was below the surface, so I reached my arm deep into the water and gripped the hood of his parka. With all my strength, I pulled him out of the water and across the qajaq, and brought him to the shore.

"By then, many people in the village had noticed what was happening, so they met me on the beach, pulled the man onto the dry ground, and took off his soaking clothes. They brought him into the warmth of a tent, wrapped him in skins, and people stripped their own clothes off so they could warm him with their body heat.

"After many hours, the man woke from his frozen sleep, and in a shiver, his eyes found me. The man said to me, "You have passed a test, now you are to become a shaman.""

Taktuq shook his head.

"The man took me away to a solemn camp not unlike this one. He lived with his wife and infant. They adopted me in a way, and he taught me many things. I learned to jump great distances, to hunt underneath the sea ice through the eyes of a seal, to communicate with the animals and to respect the spirits. Many things that man taught me ...

"After the man and his wife died, I married his daughter, Viivi. She was so beautiful. Her skin was perfect, her eyes were bright, and she was very sweet. We had our first child and she was a wonderful mother.

We travelled to the camp I had grown up in and asked to see my parents, but they had died. The leader of the village said she remembered me. She told me that my wife and I could become a part of the village. I worked with the shaman there, and we were a good team. Together, we kept the spirits happy.

"Not long after, the shaman died, and I was left there with my wife and my growing family. We had four children, beautiful children, who were smart and funny and strong. My oldest son was just learning how to become a hunter when everything went wrong."

Taktuq rubbed his eyes and went quiet. Pitu did not speak. Unsure what to do, he stayed silent, sitting forward with his elbows resting on his knees. His head felt heavy, but he could only imagine the heaviness in Taktuq as he thought of his family. Pitu could almost feel the weight seeping out of the man and wafting into the air, like the storm on his face was clearing away in order to bring a new and stronger one.

"My baby died first. We woke up one day, and the little newborn had simply stopped breathing in the night. We grieved. It happens often to a lot of newborn babies.

"The pain did not stop there, however. The next child of mine to pass away was my oldest son, who fell off a boat in the summer while I was travelling to help a shaman in another camp. The deaths continued to follow me. My wife and two other children died tragically in accidents. When I was left alone, it was revealed to me that I had angered a spirit, somehow, in my work as a shaman.

"I took nothing with me when I walked away in the middle of a winter storm. I let the wind carry me far from my home, from the people who trusted me. I had become a burden, and my presence would only bring death. Here I am now, wasting away in this beautiful place, where I am terrorized by the creatures that live here."

Pitu thought about what Taktuq had said. They were quiet, but Taktuq's body quivered with emotion. He hunched over, covering his face with his hands. The two men sat in the sunlight for a long while, silent. The air felt thick with emotion. Their thoughts shot like lightning across the sky.

"I killed my family," Taktuq said after the hour-long pause. "Don't you see that?"

"Why do you think the spirits became angry with you?" Pitu asked.

"I don't know!" he answered with his usual curtness, the emotion lessening in his voice. "All I ever did was help people!"

Pitu did not say anything. The spirits were fickle creatures, but they were never vengeful without true reason. Perhaps Taktuq was unaware that he had done something wrong by not paying the proper respect to the spirits, but Pitu had another uneasy feeling. Taktuq spoke evasively and had never finished any of his stories before now. He was angry and remained in hiding. He had done something awful, Pitu could see that. He was sure Taktuq knew that he had done something wrong.

Seeking solitude after the deaths of one's wife and children is reasonable, for a time. But as a shaman, Taktuq had responsibilities that outweighed his grief. That was one of the first things Tagaaq had taught Pitu, that it was his job as a leader to look after the people of his camp. Shamans carried this responsibility, too, because they had the power to leave the physical environment in times of stress and hardship.

"I can't believe it." Pitu laughed lightly. "I can't believe you continue to lie to me."

Taktuq fumed—*as usual*, Pitu thought—at the accusation. "I have told you everything! I killed my family. All I bring is death wherever I go. There is nothing more to it. What more do you want me to say?"

"What did you do to anger the spirits?"

"Nothing!" Taktuq shouted. "I don't know!"

"You do know," Pitu said, having nothing but calmness in him. "You know what you have done and whatever it was must have been so self-serving that you are still unable to relinquish your denial. You deny you did anything wrong, yet you know that it was your fault that your family died. So, what is it that you did?"

"You're infuriating," Taktuq muttered.

"Just say it," Pitu urged. "Tell me what you did."

"Nothing."

"Oh, great sun and earth, old man!" Pitu said in frustration, his calm quickly fading, "What did you do?"

"I already told you," Taktuq replied. "I don't know! Listen to me and understand, I have no recollection of what happened leading to their deaths." Pitu stood and paced around, his aggravation taking hold of him. The calm inside of him had snapped, leaking out the filthy feelings of rage. He needed Taktuq to say the words, needed the old man to acknowledge whatever horrible mistakes had led to the tragedy of his life. Pitu stopped in front of him, bent down and looked at the old man face to face. "Tell me what you did."

Taktuq pushed Pitu.

The young shaman didn't budge. "Tell me what you did."

"No."

"Tell me what you did."

"I did many things!" Taktuq yelled at the top of his lungs. "I stole from great men! I slept with women who were not my wife! I killed those who did not deserve it! There. Are you happy now? Are you happy to know why I am a horrible man? I do not deserve to be forgiven, young Piturniq. I do not deserve to live in a true world in a true life."

Pitu shook his head and took several steps back. "No wonder you are such a pathetic man," he said. "No wonder you are such a selfish coward. You are afraid of facing the light, you are afraid of facing the future, so you sit here with your demons."

"I sit here to keep all the others safe," Taktuq replied defensively. "When I am alone, no one can be harmed by the things I have done in my past."

"No." Pitu spat on the ground between them. "You are only self-serving here. How does this atone for what you have done? How does this fix what you have ruined? It does nothing but serve you as a hiding place in a game against the souls of those you have wronged."

"Those souls want me here." Taktuq shook his head. "I know that much."

"You disappoint me," Pitu said, shaking his head. "You are nothing more than a scoundrel who was too frightened to mend the lives he broke, especially his own. You think that you are a good man for leaving the world and sacrificing yourself to this place, but you are not a good man. Your sacrifice is nothing more than self-pity."

There was not even a hint of respect for Taktuq inside of him. Pitu scowled at the old man, so far gone from the world of the living that he didn't remember what the world was like. Pitu sat back down, adding, "You do not understand the gifts that atonement would bring."

"There should be no gifts to one who must do that. There should be no way of making amends."

"Why do you think that?"

"Bad men do not deserve such chances."

"Perhaps some bad men don't, that is true." Pitu pondered this. "But those men are the ones who do not understand and deny that they have done wrong. You are aware of your wrongdoings, you are aware of what you did and why it was bad. You are worthy of forgiveness."

Taktuq waved him off. "You are a child, Piturniq."

"And you are an old man."

"Ugh," Taktuq groaned, shaking his head, "you really are very disrespectful."

They fell into silence, each thoroughly irritated with the other, each unable to see from the other's point of view. The only sounds were that of the boiling broth that never emptied, atop the crackling fire that never died.

After a long and uncomfortable silence, Pitu decided to remember his mother's teachings. He apologized to Taktuq. He said he had spoken out of line and he was terribly sorry for all the awful things he had said and called Taktuq, all the accusations he'd thrown into the old man's face. "I neglected to remember to respect my elders, and I am gravely sorry for this. You deserve much better treatment from a student who wants to learn from you. Please forgive my foolishness."

Taktuq stood, muttering something under his breath. The old man walked, little by little, to his tent without acknowledging Pitu's apology.

16

Teach

Pitu had just finished sewing his tent together when Taktuq finally emerged from his own tent. The old man frowned at Pitu. He went around his tent and came back with a long, sturdy-looking piece of driftwood. "You can use this to hold it up. There are some good rocks behind you."

"Thank you," Pitu said. The assistance of the old man surprised him.

"Don't be so stunned. I used to help people for a living, remember?" Taktuq sighed. "I have thought about the things you have said. There is a grain of truth in your words, even though they are offensive."

Pitu nodded. He realized keeping his mouth shut might be better for their relationship.

"I have decided to teach you," Taktuq said. "Because it will get rid of you faster."

"Thank you, Taktuq."

"You never let me finish what I intend to say." The old man sighed. "I was also going to say that I have grown tired of solitude and being hunted by the creatures of this world. I would like to return home, and live the rest of my life how it was always intended. You can help me with that, I guess."

Pitu waited a moment to see if Taktuq would add more before answering, "Yes, I can."

The old man nodded, "Okay, we will start now."

The lessons Taktuq taught Pitu were unlike any others he had ever received. With Tagaaq, Pitu would learn wisdom through the elder's stories. He would learn the virtues of patience and endurance by watching what other hunters did. These lessons with Taktuq were all given in silent thought or in strange exercises.

"Close your eyes and think of your tuurngaq."

Pitu thought of the fox, its tan fur changing to white fur constantly, glowing with subtle tints of colour like the northern lights above. Tiri unfolded from a sleeping position, stood up, and padded over next to Pitu's feet. Her beady black eyes bore into Pitu, and he could see the world through her unfaltering gaze.

"What do you see?"

"I see myself in a swarm of colour," Pitu replied. "There is the grey sky beyond, except it isn't a true shade of grey, but colours that do not exist through my eyes, colours I have no name for. There are things emanating from my body, like tendrils of smoke from a fire. They take on the shapes of animals and people I know."

"Mmhmm?" he could hear the old man urge him on.

"There are seals and whales swimming around, and caribou prancing. My mother looks as though she is crying, and my little brother Atiq is not playing as he usually does. He looks as sad as my mother. My little sister Arnaapik is holding Natsivaq's youngest baby, and all of my family are crying, even my brother Natsivaq. Saima is not crying, though. Her face is serious, without a tear. I can feel the anger coming off her."

"Who is Saima?"

"My wife-to-be."

"Mm," Taktuq said. "You may open your eyes."

Pitu opened his eyes to see that it was only he and Taktuq there. Tiri had disappeared. He rubbed his eyes harshly; the switch from the vivid imagery of Tiri's eyes back to the bland colours his own eyes could see made him dizzy.

"You are very powerful, Piturniq," Taktuq said. "Did you know that?"

Pitu shrugged.

Taktuq seemed to appreciate the quiet response. He continued, "You are quite old to be learning to become a shaman, but you are quite powerful. It comes more naturally for you. Do you know what you just did?"

"I saw the world through Tiri's eyes?"

"Yes," Taktuq answered. "Through your tuurngaq, you can see more than one plane; you can see all the levels between the land of the living, the spirit world, and the land where the dead rest.

"Eventually, you will be able to transform into your tuurngaq in times of strife. It takes great desperation for this to happen. You will also need an amulet, like the foot of a fox or something from a fox, to make your communication with your tuurngaq easier when you return to the land of the living. It can be a difficult task when you are there, because there are many more things to shroud your connection."

"What was your tuurngaq?" Pitu asked, curious.

"A wolf." Taktuq smiled slightly, and then frowned. "He left me long ago."

Pitu didn't say anything. Though he had only known Tiri for a little while, he had grown fiercely attached to the spiritual fox. He wondered what it would be like, to break the bond he had with his spiritual equal, with a part of his soul.

"You may continue practising communication with your tuurngaq. It takes a great deal to create the profound bond. You must tell many stories to it, and it shall tell you stories, too." Taktuq stood, beginning to walk back to his tent. "Last night, you told her stories of your family. That is why you saw them. When you tell other stories, you will see those things, too."

Pitu set up his tent, using the beam of driftwood

Taktuq had given him to prop the skin up in a triangle. He took large rocks from around the island and lay them in the inside of the tent to anchor it down from the wind. Laying the thick caribou furs on the ground beneath the roof for bedding, he removed his clothing to lie down in pure comfort. He shut his eyes and summoned Tiri, looking at the smoke coming off his own body through the tuurngaq's eyes. The smoke showed the faces of his family billowing into the air. He said, "Let me tell you the story of Tagaaq."

The training continued. Taktuq taught Pitu to sing songs, chanting lyrics that were woven with the events of his life, such as hunting trips, near-death experiences, aiding others, and loss. The songs were about grief, hardship, success, and joy. They also constructed drums, but those would have no power.

"This is just to teach you, boy," Taktuq said. "If you are to carry a drum of real power, you will have to catch the caribou, prepare, dry, and stretch the skin of it yourself. Then it will hold your willpower inside of it. Each noise the drum makes when you beat the *katuk* on it will be a part of your voice."

He learned the dances that he had seen shamans do at qaggiq celebrations in the giant igluit, beating the katuk against the driftwood rim of the drum with slow and firm strikes. He shook his butt like a caribou, hopped around like a raven, swept his feet around like a polar bear, all while beating the drum. The songs were harder for him to create. Instead, he practised the chanting under his breath. The only song he could remember was the one he had heard his mother singing for him in his dreams.

My son has gone where the wind only knows
aijaijaa

I hear him in my dreams aijaijaa
But dark is his soul aijaijaa
He promised me he would not leave aijaijaa
But his promise has broken aijaijaa
Since he is no longer my son aijaijaa
Oh, Husband, what have you done aijaijaa
You took my boy when he was too young
aijaijaa
My son has gone where the wind only knows
aijaijaa
When he returns he will be a dark soul aijaijaa

Taktuq eventually asked what the song was, having heard Pitu whisper it as he drummed. Pitu hesitated before he spoke the lyrics aloud, nervous about what Taktuq's reaction might be. The old man went still as he listened to the words and remained silent once the song finished. It took a while for Taktuq to ask, "Where did you learn this song?"

"My mother sang it to me in a dream," Pitu answered swiftly, as if holding it in any longer would cause him to burst.

He expected Taktuq to frown and ignore him as usual. Whenever Taktuq asked him a question, he usually didn't care to wait for the answer. Instead, he would wave a dismissive hand and tell him that sometimes answering questions is unnecessary and tedious. This time, the old man tilted his head slightly. "Your mother sang this song? When?"

"Every night since I woke up in your camp."

Taktuq did not shake his head, nor did he wave a hand indifferently. The old man stayed quiet, furrowing his forehead in thought. He leaned forward, resting his elbows upon his thighs as he pondered this. Then, the old man did his signature shake of the head. "How long have you known you were a shaman?"

"Less than a year," Pitu said. "Tagaaq told me this when we were travelling to our summer camp in late spring. About a year ago I began learning how to be a good leader for the village, but shortly after, Tagaaq said that the spirits were telling him I am more than just a leader. That's when he told me I had to find you."

"But…" Taktuq stared into the distance. "Your mother knew about this longer than even Tagaaq did?"

Pitu shrugged.

"Was your father a shaman?"

"No," Pitu answered. "That line about my father in the song confuses me."

"And you promised your mother that you would not leave?" Taktuq saw Pitu shaking his head. "Then why does she say you are no longer her son?" Taktuq thought harder. "And what is it about the dark soul?"

Pitu shrugged again.

"Your mother never told you anything?" Taktuq continued. "Or your father?"

"My father often spoke about me as if I was going to leave them," Pitu admitted. "But I never understood it when he did. It makes even less sense now."

Taktuq nodded, lost in his thoughts. The movement looked foreign on the old man, his head going up and down instead of side to side. Pitu realized in that moment that he had grown quite fond of Taktuq. He was just a lonely old man with a tragic past, who'd grown bitter through his struggles. Now that the two of them were working together, Taktuq had stepped into the role of a mentor easily, and Pitu was comfortable as a student.

Taktuq said, "You know, I don't like to give you praise. Too much praise takes humility out of people. On this occasion, however, I must tell you that you are a very powerful shaman. There is a history to you that neither of us knows, and this frightens me."

Pitu had no response for that. This time he did

not respond due to a blank mind, rather than holding back brash words. He had been told about a darkness within him by Tagaaq, and through his mother's song he could hear that she could also sense the darkness. His whole life, Pitu's father had hinted to him about a future filled with mystery, and now Taktuq was beginning to piece it all together.

Pitu put his drum down and rubbed his head. An ache had formed at his temples. In the distance, he could hear a wolf howling.

Once he mastered communicating with his tuurngaq and chanting hymns that were stories and prayers, Pitu began to learn about reading bones and how to communicate with the wind. In order to read the bones, one had to be able to speak to the wind and understand its replies. To speak to bones, the joint bones of a seal were placed in a bag, not unlike a bag his own mother had. As a child, Pitu used to play with the same type of bones, asking questions and flipping the joint into the air. The answers depended on the way the bone landed; right side up meant yes, and upside down meant no.

Speaking to bones was not so different from the game he used to play as a child. He would think of a question, sometimes say it aloud, and throw several bones into the air. He would listen to the voices on the wind, and once the bones landed, he could see what the answer was. It was more difficult than his childish game, during which he would ask if he would catch a polar bear soon, or if he would marry a pretty girl. Listening to the wind and reading the bones were a study.

But that, too, did not take Pitu very long to learn. He practised until he understood it, until he could hear the voices on the wind even when he was not trying to. Taktuq seemed impressed, but the old man never told him that.

Pitu played games next, exercising his legs and body to be more manoeuvrable and flexible. He would play a hopping game to become more agile, a kicking game to jump higher, endurance games to improve his strength. He had grown up playing these games, too. They were popular for entertainment during the cold, dark winters, played in the large igluit to forget about the hunger and lack of sunlight. They also taught hunters traits that are necessary for being harvesters: strength, endurance, wit, and patience.

As he practised, Pitu's abilities became far greater than those of a regular man. He leaped farther, jumped higher, and ran nimbler. His powers as a shaman grew stronger with each exercise, allowing his lean body to contain the new-found, supernatural strength.

These sports and games made his body into a piece of soapstone, able to be carved into forms and shapes that were not his own. His legs were strong like a caribou's, his arms muscled like a polar bear, his mind as adept as a wolf's. He would practise the kneel jump, where he'd be sitting on his knees and with all his strength, spring forward, trying to gain as much distance as possible from his starting position. By the end of those practices, he was able to jump from one end of the camp to another. With high-kick jumps, Pitu was able to kick a target that was the same distance off the ground as Inukpak was tall.

Pitu was surprised by how natural he was at learning the things that made shamans have otherworldly qualities. They were remarkably normal. Things he grew up doing, but never to this extent. Still, he only needed to practise each exercise for a few days, and before long he had mastered it. It became apparent that Taktuq was also shocked, but the old man, of course, neglected to mention it.

One day, Pitu had a length of thin rope made from a strip of caribou skin. He'd scraped the fur off and stretched and dried the piece. It was to make a large necklace that would fit round the outside of his parka to show others that he was a shaman. He walked along the beach in search of animal bones or teeth for adornments, but once he returned to the world of the living, he would have to find an amulet. Outside of the spirit world, it would be difficult for Pitu and Tiri to keep track of each other. An amulet made from parts of a fox—the fur, bones, and other body parts— would help to keep them connected in the physical world.

With the help of Tiri, Pitu found a collection of bones on the beach that were small and delicate. They were dried from sitting in the sunlight for a long time, a shade of white as untarnished as a fresh snowfall. After a moment of study, he recognized them as the bones of a fox that had been dead for years.

Pitu piled rocks into a small inuksuk next to the bones to remind himself where he had placed them when he returned. He walked back to camp at a brisk pace, finding Taktuq in his usual spot by the fire. After only a day at camp, Pitu had realized that the fire never went out, and the bowl of broth never depleted. That was how the old man had survived all this time. "Taktuq," Pitu said, "I have a question."

Taktuq sighed. "What?"

"I found the bones of a fox on the beach on the other side of this island," Pitu replied. "Could I make them a part of my necklace and my amulet?"

The old man tilted his head in thought. He nodded slightly. "I suppose that would be perfect. Show me these bones."

Pitu brought Taktuq across the little island and showed him the striking bones. Taktuq squinted his eyes faintly. "I remember seeing these bones when I first arrived here."

"It is as if ..." Pitu listened to the noises around him, the voices of those who cannot be seen. He echoed what each one was telling him. "The bones have been waiting for me here all this time."

"Yes," Taktuq agreed, "I can feel it, too."

Pitu knelt down to gather the bones, picking each one up and looking closely at it. The preservation of the bones was extraordinary. They were unmarred by time or the elements, except for the clean pallor of them. With a delicate white finish, the bones reflected the sunlight, not unlike the snow. As he added the weight of the bones to his pocket, he knew exactly what each one would become—the larger ones would become new tools, like knives, harpoon heads, goggles; the teeth and the bones from the paws and tail would become decorations for his necklace; and the vertebrae from its spine he would carve into an amulet to keep in his pocket.

Foxes were typically not used or hunted. As scavengers, their stringy flesh was neither nutritious nor filling. Their fur was fluffy and warm, good for mitts or the trim around a parka hood, but so was rabbit fur; and rabbit meat had much more value. Pitu did not know why the fox bones were here, but he believed what he had said earlier, that they had been here all this time waiting for him.

Taktuq walked back to camp while Pitu picked up the bones and marvelled at each one. An uneasy feeling was growing in Taktuq's stomach. On the horizon, he could see the massive black shape of the wolf that haunted him. Until recently, it had been years since he had seen the giant creature. Now, the wolf came to check on Taktuq and the boy every time Pitu shut his eyes to sleep. The wolf never came too close to camp, and never showed up when the young shaman was awake. The old man knew that they needed to leave their camp before the wolf lost its patience.

He looked back at Pitu. The boy was almost ready, having mastered almost all of the lessons that make one into a shaman. It was like the boy had been born with wisdom as well as natural skill. In fact, sometimes it was supernatural, the way he was able to learn so quickly. Of course, that was a blessing. Soon, the creatures of the spirit world would come for them, and it was time that Taktuq quit hiding and began to fight back instead.

"Piturniq," Taktuq called back, looking over his shoulder at the young man. Pitu looked up from the bone he was examining. "I think we will begin our journey back home soon," Taktuq told him. "We will need to begin planning and preparing tonight."

Pitu smiled slightly at the thought. He missed his family. Seeing and feeling their sadness in his dreams every time he slept was beginning to take a toll on him. A memory came to mind: Tagaaq told the story of his mother quickly learning the skills to become a shaman, so that she could save the village. Perhaps that was what Pitu had been doing the whole time, too: learning and practising as much as he could, in the hopes of getting home and seeing his family soon. He wanted them to know that he was alive and well. Taktuq left as Pitu nodded his head at the old man.

As he gently held the bones and put them in his pocket, Pitu thought of the journey that lay ahead. It would be a difficult one. They would not be able to afford resting for long, and they wouldn't have any dogs to carry the supplies they would bring. *We'll pack lightly*, he thought, *and we'll move quickly*. Just as he was thinking of the trip, a shadow crossed his peripheral vision.

He looked to where the shadow had come from, and saw familiar, glowing red eyes. Pitu was jolted, and stumbled onto his butt. He was surprised to realize that the beast had been out of his mind for the past few weeks. Here it was now, huge and just as terrifying as before. He felt a pang in his leg at the memory of the wolf's jaw locking on and dragging him across the spirit world.

They stared at each other. The wolf was at the edge of the ice, seemingly unable to come onto the island. Pitu stood up slowly, grabbing the last of the fox bones. Should he run? Pitu hadn't even grabbed his harpoon or knife. Instinct told him that the wolf could come no closer.

"Taktuq!" Pitu shouted. "Taktuq!"

The old man called back, "What now?"

"There's a wolf!" Pitu yelled, growing more afraid. "The black wolf I told you about!"

"Don't bother," Taktuq replied in a monotone. "It can't come onto the island. Just leave it! It comes around sometimes, making sure that I haven't gone anywhere."

Pitu did not find that very reassuring. He walked backward toward camp, facing the beast the whole time. The wolf did not move. Tiri guided Pitu, pulling him with a voice no other person could hear. Seamlessly avoiding rocks and puddles and dents in the earth, Pitu never took his eyes off the creature until he crossed the small hill and it disappeared from sight.

17

Hardship

Pitu now understood why Taktuq had never left the island since arriving here decades ago. Uneasiness flowed through his body like an infection. Pitu remembered how mangled his leg had been, how black it had turned, and how weak he had felt when the wolf had taken him without much of a struggle. Now, with an old man and actual supplies, he was going to try to travel again?

The thought terrified him. He pulled up his fur pants to look at his legs, now healed and healthy. But there were still discoloured spots throughout his calves and shins where the wolf's teeth had punctured him.

"How will we ever make it to our home?" Pitu asked Taktuq after a long and trembling silence. His hands shook as he spoke. He hid them under his thighs, but he felt them shivering there beneath him.

"We must prepare well," Taktuq answered. "And—as evil as this world is—there are still good spirits in it. Why else would we have this island, untouchable by the spirits who mean us harm? It is because the good ones still protect us."

Pitu, having learned from the weeks he had been here with the old man, did not say anything. Instead, he waited. Without provocation, Taktuq often continued telling stories after good long silences.

"Do you remember the guide I sent for you, boy?" Taktuq asked. Pitu nodded, though he had never learned who the guide was. The guide had never shown up, and when Pitu asked Taktuq about it, the old man just became irritated. "Well, I will get it to help us for the beginning of our journey. With the wolf coming this close to our camp, I think it will remain close by. We will need help."

"Who is this guide?"
"You will see when it arrives."

———————◦◦◦———————

After a day of preparation, the men were ready to leave.
They packed their tools and dried food into slings they
could carry either by hand or with long, sturdy straps
around their foreheads to properly balance the weight
and create less strain on their muscles. They also rolled
their tents into bundles, but they would leave those
behind on the island, as the fabric would be too bulky
to carry. They had no need for the tents now anyway,
since they would not stop long enough for sleep on
the trip, and would not need them when they returned
home. Other things were to be left behind as well: the
drum that Pitu used for practice; the tools to carve
rocks, bones, and driftwood; and the pot of boiling
food would remain on the eternal fire that burned.

The night before their departure, Pitu had
carefully carved the fox bones into a necklace. Now,
he wore it around his neck and over his parka. He
could feel his own power through it. It reassured
him, knowing what he was capable of. There was an
unshakable feeling of confidence stemming from those
capabilities. That, at least, would make the journey
less terrifying.

Instead of packing the rest of the fox bones into
his sling, Pitu wrapped them carefully in caribou skin,
the thick fur cushioning them safely. Tying them up
with a strip of rope, he kept them in his front pocket
so that he would not lose the precious keepsakes.

In the morning, Taktuq and Pitu stood on the
edge of the beach, each with a pack hanging from
his back, the straps pulled across his forehead, and a
harpoon in hand. Pitu clung to the ivory snow knife in
his other hand, thinking of its usefulness when he had
been travelling alone. They were looking out at the

seasonless, white-grey expanse of the world in front of them, waiting for the guide to appear, whom Taktuq had called for the day before. Pitu himself had heard the reply. The guide had agreed to assist them, though Pitu still had no idea who it was.

Pitu was curious as to who the guide could be. Taktuq remained vague when mentioning the guide, never describing who or what it was. Pitu thought of legendary heroes in their history, stories of strong men and divine women told to him at bedtime. He never really heard the ends of the stories, but he remembered the ones about fast runners and the best and fastest qajaq-racer in the world, or the orphan who gained incredible strength after being teased by the people of his village. Could it be Kiviuq, the skillful and well-travelled hunter, coming to their aid? Then Pitu remembered that Kiviuq was sitting atop a mountain somewhere, slowly turning to stone. Once Kiviuq completely transformed into stone, the world would end.

Lost in his thoughts of meeting the people from the myths he was told as a child, Pitu wasn't paying attention to the world around him until a severed walrus head landed on the ice by the beach. Pitu gazed at the thing, the beautiful ivory tusks glistening in the sunlight, thick whiskers sticking out from its muzzle, and brown, leathery skin covering the skull. For a moment, Pitu was confused by the sudden appearance of the walrus skull. Another story sprang to his mind a moment later, and he remembered that the northern lights dancing in the sky were actually supposed to be the spirits of people who had passed away. The spirits played a game where they kicked the skull of a walrus.

Pitu looked at Taktuq, who kept his eyes on the horizon. It seemed that the old man had no care for the walrus head that seemed to have fallen out of the sky. In the distance, Pitu could hear laughter from hundreds of mouths. He followed Taktuq's gaze. Across the endless expanse of smooth and barren ice, he saw a large group of people running in their direction. Men and women and children, all dressed in beautiful clothing made from a glistening material he'd never seen before. As they approached, Pitu could see that they were made of the same essence as Tiri: ethereal and iridescent.

"Who are they?" Pitu asked.

"Those, my boy, are the northern lights," Taktuq answered with a glow in his eyes.

Taktuq's words confirmed Pitu's suspicions about the walrus head. His thoughts raced in his mind, childish excitement that the myth of the lights was true. The northern lights were the spirits of those who had passed away at peace, playing a never-ending game that looked much like soccer, kicking the head of a walrus across the sky for eternity. These thoughts were instantly overshadowed by the sudden shiver that rushed through him. My father will be there. Somehow, Pitu knew that the soul of his late father was pure enough to be a part of the most joyful element of the spirit world, the northern lights.

His eyes searched through the crowd, but there were hundreds of spirits running around, moving quicker than he could truly comprehend. Those at the front of the group had reached the end of the ice and waited. Pitu glanced at them, not recognizing who they were. They were the younger spirits, those who had died far before they should have. The young ones had red faces and were breathing heavily, huge smiles plastered across their features.

Excitement was electric in the air. Pitu felt restless, standing there at the edge of the ice, just out of reach, ready to run forward and find the spirit of his father. With a quick glance away from the northern lights to look at Taktuq, he could see that the old man was also searching the crowd for his lost loved ones.

As he looked back to the people in front of him, Pitu found himself face to face with the joyful eyes of his father. The old man, with his grey hair and beard, smiled at him. He was crying, and only a moment later, Pitu began to cry as well.

"My dearest son," his father spoke with loving softness.

"*Ataata,*" Pitu sobbed.

Without hesitation, Pitu surged forward and embraced his father, surprised that the man had a solid form despite the translucence of his spirit. Both were shaking with sobs of happiness. Neither let go for a long while.

As Pitu finally let go of his father, it registered with him that the strap of his pack had slipped from his forehead and was no longer anywhere in sight. Pitu looked at Taktuq and found the old man surrounded by children and a beautiful woman. His family. Taktuq's pack had also vanished. "Our gear," Pitu said quietly.

"The children have taken it," Ataata said. "They will carry it until we cannot take you any farther. You will have to run the whole way."

"Will you travel the whole way with me?" Pitu asked. "I have so many questions for you."

"I will run next to you for as long as I can," Ataata nodded. "But we can only diverge from our path for so long. There are many forces afoot here, my son. Those forces will catch up and correct our direction. If you can run and ask your questions at the same time, I promise to answer as well as I can."

Pitu took one last glance at Taktuq and saw tears streaming down the old man's face. Taktuq looked back at Pitu and nodded, the movement no longer seeming so strange coming from the old man. The two gazed back at their loved ones and began sprinting alongside the spirits of the northern lights.

"You must kick the walrus head!" Ataata exclaimed. "It will help you run as fast as us."

A child was running next to Pitu, avoiding the tusks as he kicked the head along. Pitu shouted

at the child to kick the ball toward him, and the child obliged, passing the head his way.

The trouble was, in all the commotion and excitement, Pitu could not avoid the tusks with the precision the others had. His toes connected with one giant tooth, and he felt a great stab of pain. *Great*, he thought, *we're not even a harpoon's length away from the island and I've already got my first injury of the journey.*

"Piturniq!" Ataata shouted. "Hurry!"

He tried again, this time kicking the walrus head with the side of his foot. He missed the tusk and sent the head farther than he thought it would go. Taktuq kicked it next, and the hundreds of soccer players passed the ball back and forth, making sure the mortals would get a hold of the head and kick it once in a while. They kept pace as they ran. Pitu and Taktuq found themselves in the centre of the group, surrounded on all sides.

As he ran, Pitu breathed in and absorbed the mirthful air that the other runners emitted. Soon, he too was filled with the same happiness that the others were, his worries vanishing. In the centre of all the commotion, his vision blurred as they ran with the supernatural speed of the northern lights. He wondered, then, if anyone in the land of the living could see them as they ran across this ice, or if he would float up into the air and become a part of the dancing lights in the sky above. All around him, the spirits began to glow in a variety of colours, most of them green. Such a luminous shade of green that it began to hurt his eyes, yet Pitu could not find it in himself to blink, afraid that he would never see such beauty or feel such joy again.

"Ataata!" Pitu called out. "Have you always known that I would be a shaman?"

"Yes!" Ataata replied. "The moment you were born, I knew that you were the next great shaman. Your mother did not want to believe me, so she tried to prevent your knowledge from growing, but I knew that you would become wise and powerful, even without being taught from an early age."

"How could you have known?"

"Sometimes you are just born with the knowledge of something, and one day that knowledge will present itself to you." Ataata laughed. "Just as we know that the sun will rise again, and the ice will thaw, I knew you would be a great one, but I did not know that until I saw you open your eyes on that cold winter night only moments after your birth."

"Why did you hide this from me?" The emotion of seeing his father was beginning to get to Pitu. He could feel it slowing him down. "Why wouldn't you have told me before you died?"

"Well, I did not know I would die so soon," said Ataata matter-of-factly, with no hint of defensiveness in his tone. "I would have told you much earlier, but your mother did not wish for you the life of a shaman. So much trouble can come of it! She didn't know what I had felt, she did not see the goodness in you!"

"Goodness?" Pitu felt his heart quicken. "All I have been told about is darkness!"

"Do you believe you have the power of darkness in you, my son?" Ataata asked. "Do you really think that you are vulnerable to dark thoughts? I never saw any darkness in my dearest son. I saw light."

Pitu continued to run alongside his father in silence. He had never felt an ounce of darkness in his soul. When Tagaaq and Anaana had both said they felt it in him, he felt upset that they believed that of him. Now his father, the biggest influence in his life, said the complete opposite. "Thank you." Pitu spoke quietly, between heavy breaths.

"I love you, my son," Ataata said. "Tell your mother that I love her, too."

Then they ran in silence, kicking a walrus head in a game of soccer among the spirits of the dead.

Pitu was surprised by how long he ran without tiring. Taktuq also kept up, unyielding in his pace. They gained most of their energy from kicking the head. They ran for hour upon hour. It was unclear how far they had gone. With a glance behind him, Pitu could see that they had come far enough that they could no longer see the summer island. Ahead there was nothing but a vast expanse of barren ice. Even Inukpak's mountains were not yet visible in the distance.

The horizon being invisible could have made it difficult to decipher how far they had gone. The sky was a shade of white that blended with the snow on the ice. There were no rocks or patches of land to mark the way. For all he knew, they could have gone around the mountains, or perhaps there was a hill completely covered in snow that was invisible in the whiteout.

In his peripheral vision, Pitu saw strange movement to the left of the crowd. The spirits began a collective, eerie shriek. Ataata was shrieking with the others, so Pitu looked to Taktuq for answers. Looking to his left, he caught sight of Taktuq, but the old man's gaze was trained elsewhere.

Pitu followed his gaze. He saw what was making the spirits scream.

A pack of dark wolves were sprinting alongside the group. Pitu looked to his right and saw another pack. They were the same ones he had encountered when he first arrived—the human features, the sleek fur, and the laughter. Pitu's heart pounded painfully and his vision tunnelled slightly, his racing blood making him have a small panic attack.

It didn't take long for him to spot the giant black wolf. It seemed more sinister than ever, the fur of its neck sticking up in pointy tufts of rage, the red eyes glowing and teary. As the other wolves began creepily cackling, the black wolf snarled viciously, the noise echoing even among the shrieks of the spirits and over the flat expanse.

Though they had not stopped running, they had slowed significantly. The wolves were darting into and out of the crowd of spirits, lunging for their legs with each attack. Pitu knew then that it would not be long before the spirits of the northern lights would turn away and abandon the two shamans.

Thinking that he would soon be gone forever, Pitu took the moment to just look at his father and admire him. Ataata's face was brown and weather-beaten, with a lighter area across his eyes where his snow goggles had protected him from the reflection of the sun on the snow's surface for years and years. He had silver hair, eyebrows, and beard. Pitu thought of the qualities that had made Ataata such a respectable man. He had never disrespected his wife's wishes and had taught his sons every trick one needed to know to be a great hunter. To his daughters, he showed endless love and kindness, even spoiling them a bit.

The spirits had stopped shrieking and were instead trying to increase their pace. Ataata took hold of Pitu's arm to guide him, perhaps sensing that Pitu was no longer paying much attention to the path.

"Ataata," Pitu said softly. "You must go."

"We can take you farther, my son." Ataata shook his head. "We can keep—"

Just then, a wolf leaped out and locked its jaws on the leg of a spirit, dragging it away from the group. The wolf screamed with mirth at the catch, gnawing at the spirit of the young boy it had caught. The spirits stopped running completely and began their combined screaming again, chanting in unison. Chants that sounded purposeful.

Pitu looked at Taktuq for guidance, but the old man looked hopeless and frightened. Though the shrieks of the northern lights seemed to ward off the wolves, how long would it last? The commotion all around was confusing, making Pitu feel dizzy. He summoned Tiri to his side, looked at the fox, and called to her, "Send help!"

Tiri bolted away from the scene, shooting from the crowd and into the distance like a flash of lightning.

Pitu strode over to Taktuq. In spite of the panic he felt in his chest, he tried to pull everyone together. Silently, he was thankful for the terrible days he had travelled alone in the wilderness of the spirit world, for now it made him think quickly and strategically. Pitu took hold of Taktuq by both his shoulders and shook the old man. "Think, Taktuq!" Pitu yelled. "We must do something!"

"The wolves will never stop!" Taktuq cried.

"So?" Frustrated, Pitu shook the man again. "Stop being your cowardly self! Perhaps the wolves will never stop hunting us, but we can fight them and evade them until we leave here, or die trying!"

Taktuq blinked and firmly locked his wet eyes with Pitu's. The old man nodded. "Send Tiri to get help. She will know who can help us!"

"I've already done that."

"Then we shall wait." Taktuq took a few strides to the left, and found his pack at the feet of a shrieking hunter's spirit. He took out his pointed harpoon and sharp knife. Turning around and facing Pitu, the two looked like reflections of each other, like Pitu was glimpsing his future self and Taktuq his past. Taktuq looked at his wife, who still chanted with the others. Pitu saw her incredible beauty, and he thought of Saima back at home.

I will see her again, Pitu thought. *I will tell her I love her again.*

Just as Pitu thought of this, Taktuq was saying the same things to his wife and children. He left them to their private moment, even if the spirits seemed unable to see past their shrieking chants. Pitu went back to his father and embraced the man who could not return the warmth.

Around them, the wolves were running in circles and jumping back or leaping in the air. They were frenzied over the noise. The black wolf remained still, however, its gaze fixed on Pitu. Pitu felt as though the creature could stare into his soul. He made sure his grip on his weapons was firm, afraid that somehow the wolf would dart through the crowd and attack him specifically.

A moment later, Tiri reappeared. She circled around the northern lights and the wolves at an unnatural speed, kicking up snow in dusty flashes. The black wolf tore its gaze from Pitu and followed the fox, but Tiri was too fast to be seen.

Then a roar broke the chanting of the northern lights. The wolves stopped their confused frenzy. The black wolf stopped its pursuit of the fox. Over a hill—that Pitu hadn't even known was right next to them—a herd of caribou flanked by grey and white wolves appeared. Pitu instantly recognized Inukpak's pets. They were no longer the tame creatures of the camp in the mountains, begging for treats from the giant. Now they ran with ferocity, the wolves and the caribou together sprinting toward the dark wolves. There was no way that the giant's pets had made the roaring sound. Pitu knew that Inukpak must not be far away.

Behind the animals came Inukpak, clad in a parka with the bones of bowhead whales sewn all over it. She held a sturdy-looking rib bone in each hand as clubs to fight with. The ribs were curved and pointed at the ends, sharpened along the edge. Two glittering white polar bears were at her sides, running with great speed toward the great black wolf.

If Inukpak's appearance had surprised the wolf as it had Pitu, the wolf did not show it. Leisurely, the beast took one last glance at Pitu and adjusted its stance to face Inukpak's polar bears as they approached. The bears were a blinding shade of white, ropes of muscle lining their limbs and bodies. They ran with a ferocious grace.

Inukpak roared again, loud and anguished. Her eyes were red from what looked to be sleepless grief. She swung her giant clubs at the wolves, slicing some in half, making the others run away in horror.

The northern lights halted their chanting. Next to Pitu, Ataata shouted, "Run!"

A spirit kicked the walrus head toward Taktuq. The old man kicked it to Pitu and the game of soccer began once more.

"Thank you, Inukpak!" Pitu yelled as he ran past the giant.

She fought the black wolf while her animals dealt with the smaller wolves. Inukpak glanced at Pitu, winked a bloodshot eye at him, and said, "Run, my little hunter! Return to your loves!"

Pitu felt his heart break. Though he had been her prisoner, she had taken such good care of him, feeding him caribou and fish and seal. He thought of what Taktuq had said weeks ago—*Inukpak is the last giant. She does become very lonely.* All the giant wanted was a companion, someone to share her life with.

Pitu ran away, feeling the warmth of water stinging his eyes. As they crossed over the top of the hill, he stole one last glance behind, seeing the blood-soaked legs of the giant. She fought relentlessly, but the black wolf did, too. Unable to wait any longer, Pitu continued running, and soon he was too far away to see anything but the snow that had been turned up by the footprints of hundreds of fleeing feet.

18

Light

The northern lights dulled as they began to slow down after an eternity of racing from the danger. Now that they were coming to a stop, Pitu finally noticed the green, blue, and purple glow that shone around them as they ran. They were panting, making the air turn hazy. The mountains were much closer now, still too far away to reach in a short amount of time, but close enough that Pitu recognized their shape. They were the mountains where Inukpak had brought him all those weeks ago.

"Son," Ataata said, "we must leave you now."

Pitu nodded, resigned. "I am most fortunate to have seen you, Ataata."

They embraced with overwhelming emotion, wiping the wetness from their eyes. Ataata gave an apologetic smile. Morosely, Pitu mirrored him. They said their goodbyes, and soon, the northern lights began to leave, fading into the distance, their departure leaving a sour taste in the back of Pitu's throat. They watched each other until his father was lost in the crowd of spirits. Soon, they floated into the sky, quickly disappearing.

A moment lingered while the two shamans stared after the northern lights, treasuring the time they had had with the dead. Their silence started out tensely, swiftly transforming into anxious restlessness. They wiped their faces, picked up their packs, which the spirits had left for them, and began walking toward the mountains.

Tiri appeared immediately, relaying silently that the two shamans were going in the wrong direction. "She says we have to go that way," Pitu said, pointing in a direction parallel to the mountains that was just flat ice.

Taktuq did not argue. The old man was too emotional to be his grumpy self. They went on their way, adjusting their direction and walking at a steady, brisk pace. Neither of them knew if Inukpak could kill the beast that pursued them, nor how long she could hold it off if she couldn't kill it.

Pitu recognized his surroundings now, thankful that running with the northern lights had brought them most of the way back toward the land of the living. Even after weeks at Taktuq's camp on the summer island, Pitu could see the windswept mounds of his footsteps. The shelter he had been sleeping in when he was stolen by Inukpak was still there, sturdy against all odds.

"It took me four days and four nights to reach this spot, Taktuq," Pitu told him while they marched. "I didn't have supplies then."

"You were not trained as a shaman at that time, either," Taktuq replied. "You did not have your tuurngaq to alert you to danger, or the ability to hear the voices in the wind, or the ability to jump across large rivers ... that last one, I think, will be most helpful."

And then Taktuq smiled. He actually smiled.

Whereas the encounter with the northern lights had left Pitu feeling a sense of agony, it had rejuvenated the old man. Pitu mistook the emotional silence as sadness, but now, he could see that Taktuq was overjoyed.

"Taktuq, I have never seen you so happy," Pitu remarked.

"All these years I have been here, Piturniq," Taktuq spoke softly, "and I was too frightened to see my family again. It was my fault they died and I assumed they would despise me for this."

"But they didn't?"

"No." Taktuq's smile widened. "They forgave me."

Pitu did not say anything. They walked on with lightness in the air. Now, the silence they were in was comfortable, even a bit cheerful. Pitu could see now that they were moving at a much faster pace than he had when he was alone. Tiri remained at his side, nose in the air to sniff out any danger.

It was peaceful.

Time seemed to be at a standstill. The sky never changed from its dull shade of white to a dark night sky. All that could be heard was their harsh breath and the crunch of the hard snow under their feet. Nothing changed in their surroundings, except when they glanced at the adjacent mountains and saw how far they had walked.

Occasionally, one would say something that made the other laugh, then they would continue in their silence.

Hours had passed when the two finally took a short break. Having already passed the remains of the iglu Pitu had built while running away from the wolves, they were now stopped next to one of the haphazard igluit Pitu had built along the way, before he knew the wolves existed. Taktuq took out thin strips of dried caribou that had been bundled into a bag made of dried skin. For water, they simply melted snow in their mouths.

"It took us less than a day to reach this spot, but on my own it took me two days between here and the snow shelter we began at," Pitu stated, impressed by their speed. "Perhaps we will reach our destination much faster than I thought."

"Time and distance are different here, Piturniq," Taktuq said. "Before, when you lacked your powers, it took you much longer. The land did not feel your power, so it did not assist you. Now, it can sense what makes you different from a regular mortal. It senses your ability to go beyond because you have learned the ways of shamanism."

They finished eating and packed up their things. Each grabbed a handful of snow before continuing their walk toward the spot where Pitu's whole journey had begun all those weeks ago.

19

Sacrifice

The two shamans stood before the large, jagged shards of ice that loomed tall above them. Pitu felt their ominous energy in the air. The body of the qallupilluq that Pitu had killed was gone; the snow was clean, with no signs of the struggle that had happened here all those weeks ago.

Before venturing into the menacing path through the shards of ice, Pitu and Taktuq took out the dried meat again and chewed on it for a while, building up the nerve to continue on. The problem was that sitting there, just outside the field of jagged ice, seemed to make them more nervous as the seconds passed by. They ate in silence, keeping an eye out for any strange movements.

Unable to stand the quiet any longer, Pitu said, "We are so close. Just beyond that hill is our destination."

Taktuq nodded. "Let's rest just a little while longer."

So, they rested, eating snow and caribou meat. Tiri vanished, exploring the area while they waited, in search of dangers that might be close by. The two shamans spoke to each other of their homes. To Pitu, home was where his family was; it was the knowledge that he could hunt and provide for his family. For Taktuq, he still thought of the summer island as his home, where he felt at least some form of peace from his sorrows.

"Now that you've seen your family again," Pitu began, "your sorrows must have disappeared?"

"It is not so simple," Taktuq replied. "I lived with that sorrow for years, Piturniq. Though I feel the weight of my grief and guilt lightened, it is still there. It is still something that I have within me. Living alone on that island helped me keep the feelings at bay until you arrived."

Pitu left it at that, not wanting to upset Taktuq into an outburst of annoyance. Once Taktuq returned to the world they belonged to, he'd feel differently. He'd feel at peace again. For now, Pitu was surprised by how long it had been since anything strange had happened.

Unfortunately, Tiri reappeared only a moment later with her aura glowing red to alert them of danger. Pitu cursed himself. He had jinxed the peace.

"Taktuq, we have to go!" Pitu grasped the old man's arm and pulled him up from where he sat on the ice. "Something is coming."

Before their very eyes, the familiar black shape appeared on the horizon. The wolf was racing toward them, growing larger by the second.

Without another word, the two turned and ran into the path through the shards of ice, leaving their packs behind. Pitu held only his harpoon now, having laid the knife down while they were eating. Taktuq was the same, holding only his harpoon. A piece of dried caribou meat stuck out of his mouth, as if he refused to spit it out.

Weaving through the ice was more difficult than the last time he'd come here. The cracks were larger, the jutting shards closer together, squeezing them into close quarters. They had to move slowly, stretching their legs over the cracks, bending low to avoid ice that stuck out sharply.

They moved through efficiently. That is, until Pitu looked down into a particularly large crack in the ice, and he saw faces staring up at him.

Pitu screamed at the sight. They were grey faces with sharp teeth and bulbous eyes. He recognized the qallupilluit. This time, there were dozens of them.

Pitu jumped, launching himself from the crack. But curiosity had propelled Taktuq forward, and he leaned over the crack to see what was there.

A long and bony hand reached out of the crack, the sharp claws slashing at the old man. The claws tore a cut into the front of Taktuq's parka. Panicking, he jumped forward without aim, and he crashed directly into Pitu, sending them both crashing to the ground.

"Go, go, go!" they shouted simultaneously.

The wolf's howl pierced the air. The wailing of the qallupilluit rose in answer.

Pitu was already frightened, but hearing the communication between the wolf and the qallupilluit made his blood run cold. He hadn't thought that the creatures would be able to understand each other.

Neither Pitu nor Taktuq lingered to see what would happen. Pitu summoned Tiri before them and asked for guidance through the field of ice. Tiri obliged, skirting off at a pace that was efficient and avoided the larger cracks.

·Despite the eerie howls and the wailing, the two of them followed Tiri effortlessly. Hiking through the labyrinth of ice was not easy; however, the terror running through them made their movements brisk. They did not move with grace. In fact, they moved sloppily, slipping and stumbling, but they recovered quickly. At one point, their harpoons were too long to pass through a particularly tight squeeze. If they'd had the time, they would have been able to simply crawl through, with their harpoons in hand, but that just wasn't the case. They let the harpoons go in hopes of making a quick escape.

Pitu could almost feel the breath of the creatures behind them on his neck. He raced for his life. Suddenly he was out of the ice. He almost fell forward, but righted himself. Taktuq did the same. Without hesitation, they began the trek up the hill, running and falling and running again.

They had only taken a dozen steps when the wolf emerged from the field of ice, flanked by many qallupilluit who had climbed from their homes in the ice cracks. Now, the shamans were weaponless and had no shelter. Their enemy was going to win.

"Pitu, jump," Taktuq said. "Jump as far as you can. It might not work, but it's our only hope. Perhaps we can make it to the other side of the hill if we jump far enough."

Pitu did not waver. He leaped, launching himself only a few feet away. He shook his head. It was a warm-up, he told himself. Once Taktuq jumped, much farther than Pitu had, they continued their hurdles forward, but Pitu was not jumping as far as he thought he could, and the creatures were closing in on him.

He tried, though. He didn't stop trying.

Almost at the top, he felt jaws locking on his leg. Memories surfaced in his mind, the same pain in his leg as before. How long had the wolf clenched its teeth on this very same leg? How long had it taken for Pitu's leg to turn black? He hadn't known how much time had passed, how long he had been unconscious. His fright returned, thinking of that aimless, never-ending trek the wolf had taken him on.

"Taktuq!" Pitu shouted. "Find my mother and tell her I am sorry!"

The wolf began to yank Pitu away aggressively. The qallupilluit reached toward him, digging their sharp claws into the skin of his face and neck, puncturing his chest and limbs through his parka. He felt blood rise from the various wounds, but the gashes were shallow, only cuts on the surface, as if the creatures only wanted to mark him, not injure him.

The wolf stopped heaving only a short distance down the hill, leaving him lying on the ground. It looked up at Taktuq, leering at the old man. What was it trying to do? Provoke him? Pitu stayed still, not sure if his movements would cause another act of aggression from the wolf or the qallupilluit. Confusion swarmed through Pitu's mind. What was the wolf doing?

And then Pitu listened. And he could hear it all.

The wolf was Taktuq's tuurngaq.

And then it made sense. The wolf hunting him, always pursuing him through the land of spirits. The wolf taking him on a seemingly aimless trek when really it had taken him straight to Taktuq. The wolf was not just hunting him, it was making sure that Pitu made it to Taktuq.

He kept listening to what the spirits were saying, what the wind needed to tell him.

The spirits of the world needed a life. They needed a life to send another back to the land of the living. They needed Pitu's life in order to send Taktuq back to the mortals, or they needed Taktuq's life to send Pitu back.

The wolf screamed through the air. Pitu should not have been able to hear it, but he could. It screamed to Taktuq, *Kill him! Kill him and we will be free again!*

"No!" Taktuq shouted. "No, you have no power over me!"

Tiri ran in circles, disordered and unsure of what to do. For once, she did not know how she could help Pitu. He concentrated on what the wolf was screaming through the air. It was faint, since other shamans are not supposed to be able to understand or hear a tuurngaq that is not their own, but because the bond between Taktuq and the wolf was weak, Pitu was able to hear the wolf.

I cannot kill the boy! The wolf's voice was not like Taktuq's. It was furious and frustrated, as opposed to Taktuq's, which was bitter and tired. *It has to be you!*

Taktuq answered with fortitude in his voice, "I will not kill him."

The wolf barked in its frustration.

Pitu thought of ways to escape, but there were

no other options. He had nothing to fight off the qallupilluit, and even if he could get away from them, the wolf was too strong and too quick to evade. The wolf might not be able to kill Pitu, but it could still maul him, it could still tear him apart and torment him.

Taktuq took tentative steps down the hill. He held his arms wide, surrendering himself to the wolf.

The voices in the wind speculated, echoing the confusion Pitu felt. *What in the world is going to happen?*

"Amaruq," Taktuq spoke softly, in the gentlest tone Pitu ever heard the old man use. "I have not seen you for so long."

The wolf, Amaruq, grumbled.

"We have been parted for decades, Amaruq."

Because you are weak, Amaruq said. *You are too weak to embrace your true power.*

"I do not want my power," Taktuq said, "if it means that those I love will die."

The wolf shook its head angrily. Pitu almost laughed. It moved the same way Taktuq did, sharing his favourite gesture. They were incredibly similar, now that Pitu knew they were one and the same. However, they warred with each other, the old man clinging to his last bit of humanity, the wolf embracing darkness.

Taktuq lowered his arms, stopped his slow steps forward. The wolf tensed. Taktuq rested his hands on his hips.

Before Pitu realized what was happening, before he remembered that Taktuq had a belt with a slot in which he rested his snow knife, the old man pulled out his knife in a swift movement. Amaruq lunged forward, sensing what was happening.

Taktuq took the knife, and firmly thrust it into his own abdomen.

Amaruq cried out at the sight, feeling the pain that Taktuq suddenly felt. Pitu screamed, shocked at what he was seeing. Amaruq began to dim and shrink, no longer able to stay corporeal as Taktuq's life quickly began to fade. Pitu felt the grasp of the qallupilluit weaken in shock as the wolf slowly faded away. With a surge of energy, Pitu stood and launched himself out of the qallupilluit's reach and was by Taktuq's side in only a second.

"Taktuq!" Pitu shouted.

"Piturniq," Taktuq gasped, "thank you."

20

Alive

now swarmed around Piturniq.

He stared at Taktuq, clutched at the old man's body, holding him with all the strength that was left within him. Tears seeped out of Pitu's eyes, sobs and screams lurched from his throat. The life drained from Taktuq's body quickly. None of Pitu's cries for the old man to stay awake were heard, and the old man's breathing sputtered to a stop.

The storm around Pitu thickened, making the qallupilluit disappear entirely. Though the strength of the wind attempted to dislodge Pitu's grip on Taktuq's lifeless body, he clung on. Unable to part the two, the winds shrugged, and brought both bodies—one living, and one dead—back to the mortal world.

Hours passed, Pitu knew, but it felt like only a moment. He lay his face on Taktuq's motionless chest as the winds bit into his cheeks, wet with tears. In what felt like the blink of an eye, an infinite amount of time passed.

Once the wind slowed and Pitu looked up from Taktuq's body, he saw the fresh tracks of a dogsled just in front of him, and he could see a man a far distance away, standing patiently at a hole in the ice, waiting for a seal.

"Ai!" Pitu yelled. "Help!"

The hunter's profile straightened. Without hesitation, whoever it was began to sprint toward Pitu. He looked around at the setting, noticing three more hunting parties and a group of men approaching on dogsleds.

In no time, Pitu was surrounded by the hunters.

"It's Piturniq!" said a voice.

"Where did he come from?"

"He's been lost for weeks."

"Natsivaq!" said another. "It's Piturniq!"

Pitu stared at the man who was running toward him, the first one he had seen. The man's shape became more apparent and familiar. The winds told him it was his brother.

He looked down at Taktuq's body, but it was gone. Pitu was alone on the ground, surrounded by people he had known his whole life, but could not recognize. They asked questions about where he had been and what had happened and why he had been gone for so long. Pitu couldn't answer. His throat hurt from the shrieks of his grief, and his body hurt from the journey. His head swam with the events that had happened only moments ago, and his body knew that he could finally rest.

Confusion ran rampant through him, and heartbreak reminded him of his mortality, his longing for his family. Tiri appeared on the outskirts of the hunters, calm and serene.

Natsivaq finally reached them. The man fell to his knees at the sight of his firstborn child. His cheeks glistened as he crawled toward Pitu and embraced him. "_Irniq,_" Natsivaq moaned, "My son."

Their cries of joy and disbelief could be heard back in the camp, that lay far in the distance, where children stopped playing and ran into their igluit to tell their parents what they had heard over the wind. Parents and elders came out and waited for the hunting party to return with whatever they had caught. It was time, many of them thought, that they found joy rather than grief for the first time in weeks. Pitu's mother reluctantly came out of her iglu with her two youngest children, Atiq and Arnaapik. Her face was tearstained as she looked at the horizon, waiting for news of what the hunters had found.

Pitu slept soundly as he was brought to the village on a dogsled. Through the bumps of the uneven ice and over cracks that did not have qallupilluit in them, through the biting winds and the barking dogs, he slept without waking and, thankfully, dreamt of nothing.

As they arrived at the village, Pitu woke from his sleep and saw the faces of those he loved. A young boy ran toward them, and Pitu recognized his little brother Atiq. The reckless little boy whooped and shouted as he approached. He ran the whole way until he was next to the sled, changing directions to run alongside. Pitu could see the disbelief in Atiq's face, the grief quickly erasing from his features. Only a moment later, Arnaapik was running along, too. Tears ran down her face. He knew that his mother would be waiting on the tips of her toes for them to arrive at the edge of the welcoming party, but he wondered if Saima would be there, too, waiting for her lost husband-to-be. Pitu felt anticipation in his stomach.

He could feel the tears on his cheeks. He still mourned Taktuq, but his heart was breaking from the happiness of seeing the faces of those he had dreamt of for weeks. In those dreams, his family had been despondent and grieving. To finally see their faces showing incredible happiness was enough to make his breath get caught in his throat, unable to pass the lump that had lodged there.

The sled stopped moving. Pitu craned his neck and saw the small frame of his mother. She strode forward cautiously, unsure of whether she should believe that her son had been found and returned safe and sound. Pitu raised himself off the sled, stood in front of the crowd of onlookers, all of whom were staying at a safe distance.

"Anaanangai," Pitu spoke softly. He splayed his arms wide to embrace her. Anaana reached him and fell into his outstretched arms. Her cries were silent and heavy, sucking in deep breaths before each quiet sob. She clutched at Pitu's arms, lightly brushed her fingers over his face, buried hers into his parka.

"My son," she said in a slight voice. "Your parka is ruined. I must make you a new one."

"Yes." Pitu smiled, the normality of what she had said making him feel completely at home again. "I have many stories to share. Ataata wanted me to tell you he loves you."

Anaana's eyes glowed. They were interrupted as the people of the camp came forward to see and speak to Pitu, asking him questions about what had happened and where he had gone. Suddenly overwhelmed, Pitu could feel all his weariness again.

"I need sleep," he told them.

Pitu was guided to his mother's iglu by his whole family. He scanned the crowd of onlookers, faces he recognized, but he did not see Saima. *Perhaps*, he thought, *she is sleeping*. Once he was in the privacy of his mother's iglu, he crawled onto the bedding to sleep comfortably for hours and hours without a single worry.

When he awoke, there were three people sitting in the iglu in front of him. Tagaaq sat on the bedding right next to him, the elder's legs folded underneath him. Taktuq stood near the entrance of the iglu, his head high and proud, the storm that had raged across his face was now calm, and he looked open and relaxed. Lastly, a woman tended to the qulliq, bent over and focused. Pitu assumed it was his mother, hunching over the small, steady flames to keep the light from going out.

The woman, sensing Pitu stirring, looked over. Her eyes were blank, pupils gone grey and irises gone to a shade of blue comparable to melting ice. Though he had never seen this woman before, Pitu knew instinctively that this was Tagaaq's mother, Angugaattiaq, the shaman who had saved the ancestors of this camp from starvation by sacrificing her eyesight.

Of course, Pitu had realized he was dreaming as soon as he saw Taktuq. He sat up in bed and waited for one of them to speak. The iglu was cold in their presence, as if the ice from the afterlife was sticking to their bodies. Tagaaq was the one who spoke first.

"Piturniq, we are overjoyed that you have returned," he said. "You are much stronger than we could have anticipated."

Taktuq nodded in agreement. The motion no longer seemed strange coming from the old man. He appeared much more confident and content now, not so haunted by his past. "I hear they call you 'Piturniq the Great Hunter.'" Taktuq laughed quietly in his thoughts. "Well, I suppose they will call you many names from now on."

"Ai, that is true." Tagaaq laughed, too. "All the

hunters will be jealous and all the women will swoon."

Taktuq sniggered. "And children will be scared of you."

"Enough," said Angugaattiaq, chuckling between her words, "we came here for a purpose. To prepare him, not to tease him."

"Yes," the two men said in unison. Tagaaq carried on, "We have come to tell you that you are now a man of great power."

"Word will spread fast, Piturniq the Great Hunter," Taktuq elaborated, chuckling as he called Pitu by his famous nickname. "You must prepare yourself for all the work you will have to do."

"Yes." Angugaattiaq had a soft, authoritative voice that commanded respect. "The spirits will tell you stories of turmoil. People will travel from far and wide to see and speak to you, and evil spirits will seek you out. It will be quite exhausting. You must not let it tire you."

Pitu did not know what to say. He was talking to the spirits of two dead shamans and the spirit of a living man. It was surreal, and a little disturbing. Though he had encountered many strange things over the past month or so, this was something he just could not really wrap his head around. They were not only speaking to him, they were also making jokes between pieces of advice.

Angugaattiaq continued, "I hope you're ready … but from what Taktuq has told me, it seems that you are more than able."

"I may have exaggerated slightly," Taktuq said. As if the situation was not strange enough, Taktuq's confidence and joking attitude perplexed Pitu the most. "You are a wise man, but you are also annoying and disrespectful."

"Oh my, Taktuq." Pitu joined in the laughter. "I've never heard you speak so casually."

"I woke up and saw the faces of my family,"

Taktuq smiled. "I have no more reason to feel the terrible way I felt for so long."

That comment sent the four into a moment of silence. It was filled with a sense of contentment. They all sighed in unison. Angugaattiaq stood from her position. "We must leave you now, Piturniq."

"Wait," Pitu said. A sense of urgency rushed through him, questions popping into his head. "What kind of work will I have to do?"

"Tagaaq is still here to teach you, young hunter," Angugaattiaq answered. "And your tuurngaq will guide you. The spirits will advise you. You must only listen."

With one last solemn nod toward Pitu, Taktuq left the iglu and Angugaattiaq followed. Pitu's eyes felt heavier as Tagaaq said one last thing.

"My dear boy, we have a lot ahead of us."

Opening his eyes, Pitu knew that this time he was not dreaming. Atiq and Arnaapik had both fallen asleep against Pitu's side, their arms embracing his bare chest. Anaana sat at the qulliq, as she usually did, except that she firmly gripped his leg with one hand, as if she thought that her hold of him would keep him from disappearing.

Pitu kissed his younger siblings on their foreheads, and coaxed them to let go of him so that he could get up. Arnaapik let go without hassle, and turned onto her side to continue sleeping. Atiq cried and wouldn't let go until Pitu promised he would not leave the camp.

Pitu made his way over to his mother. They sat close together, Anaana looking away from the qulliq and taking hold of her son's hand. She asked, shyly and quietly, "So, you saw my husband?"

Pitu nodded. "Yes, he was running with the northern lights."

"That man." Anaana's eyes watered, unsure whether she believed what Pitu had told her or not. She shook her head a little. "He warned me about you and I never listened."

"Do you still think that I have darkness inside of me?" he asked, afraid of the answer.

"I never thought there was darkness in you, my son." Anaana wiped the tears from her eyes. "I was frightened. I felt the darkness of another soul inside of you. I tried not to believe in it, but as you became a greater hunter, the darkness I felt around you also seemed to become greater. I knew that you were a man of light, my dear son, but the spirits are fickle creatures, and sometimes they change a man's lightness into darkness. Once you disappeared, I was afraid that my fears had come true and you were gone forever."

Pitu didn't say anything. He embraced his mother as she cried. She had spoken with honesty, but Pitu couldn't stop thinking of the song she had sung to him every night for weeks. As thoughts of his time in the other world came to mind, Pitu felt enclosed and short of breath. He got dressed in his ruined parka, pants, and boots. "I am going to speak to Tagaaq," he told her.

When he left the iglu, however, he did not go to Tagaaq's iglu. He made his way to a string of dogs, untethered to any of the sleds. They recognized his scent and stature instantly. Pitu kneeled next to the dogs, letting them come and lick his face.

He stayed with them for quite a while before he felt the presence of another person behind him. Turning around, Pitu saw Saima, her cheeks wet from tears. She walked over to him, kneeled next to him, and reached out her hands to his face.

"You have scars," she whispered.

He nodded, unable to find any words. She was just as beautiful as ever, her dark hair braided in two plaits, her face covered in the tattoos that represented maturity and womanhood. She had not had those when he'd left, only the thin double V on her forehead. Now, there were the same thin V-shapes on her cheeks, reaching out from her ears to point at her nose, and six straight lines on her chin, connecting from her jawline to her lower lip.

"You were gone for so long," she said, leaning her forehead onto his shoulder.

"I missed you," he said after the long, intimate moment. "I thought of you every time I thought I would not make it back home."

Saima nuzzled closer for a second, then moved back quickly, like it wasn't allowed, which it actually wasn't. "I didn't want to, Piturniq, okay? I didn't want to."

"What are you talking about?" he asked, though he had a small sense of what she was about to say.

"We thought you were dead, Piturniq." Saima's voice broke. "They thought we would never see you again, even though Tagaaq said you were alive, no one believed him ..."

He didn't say anything.

"I am married to another man," she cried. She hardly breathed as her words began bursting from her mouth. "I didn't want to marry him, but my parents made me. My father and brothers were not catching enough seals to feed us, so when Ijiraq offered to marry me once again, they said yes. Even though you are here now, they won't allow me to break the marriage to be with you. They do not want to disrespect him twice."

She cried into her hands. Pitu reached out and rubbed her shoulders until she leaned forward for him to hug her. "It's okay," Pitu said. "I understand."

Jealousy coursed through him. He wanted to march to Amarualik's iglu and demand they cancel the arrangement with the new husband, but that would be disrespectful and greedy. Instead, he hugged Saima until her sobs subsided, and she laid her nose and mouth on his cheek and inhaled deeply. She lingered there for a moment, the last time they would be able to talk to each other honestly and privately.

"I still love you," Pitu whispered into her hair. He inhaled, too, kissing her cheek the same way she did. "I'll always love you."

She stood and walked away, leaving him with the dogs. Miki, once the runt of the litter, came and lay down, resting her head in his lap. Pitu looked up at the dark sky, seeing the northern lights dancing above. He thought of Taktuq's sacrifice, of Ataata's courage and faith in him, of all those spirits that had helped him in his journey, of Inukpak the lonely giant. And he remembered all those who run in the sky.

Glossary

Aapak	[ah-puck]	Name.
ai	[aye]	Greeting/affirmation.
aijaijaa	[eye-ya-e-ya]	A traditional musical refrain.
alianait	[a-lee-a-nite]	An expression of joy.
Amaruq	[a-ma-rook]	Name, also means "wolf."
Amarualik	[a-ma-roo-ah-lick]	Name.
amauti pl. amautiit	[a-mow-tee, pl. a-mow-teet]	A woman's parka—usually with a pouch in the back to carry a baby, and a large hood to cover the heads of the mother and baby from the cold.
anaana	[a-naa-na]	Mother.
anaanaapiingai	[a-naa-naa-pee-ng-eye]	"My beloved mother."
anaanangai	[a-naa-naa-ng-eye]	"Hello, my dear mother."
Angugaattiaq	[a-ng-oo-got-tee-ak]	Name.
Apita	[a-pee-ta]	Name.
Arnaapik	[ahn-naa-pick]	Name, meaning "beloved young girl."
Arnatsiaq	[ahr-nut-see-ak]	Name, inspired by a prominent family from Iglulik, Nunavut.
ataata	[a-taa-ta]	Father.
Atiq	[ah-tick]	Name, meaning "name."

Atiqanngituq	[a-tee-ka-ng-ee-took]	Name, meaning "nameless."
avani	[a-va-nee]	"Go away," or "shoo."
hai	[hi]	The Inuktitut equivalent of "what?"
iglu pl. igluit	[ee-glue, pl. ee-glue-eet]	A dome-shaped house made with blocks of snow.
Iglulik	[ee-glue-lick]	A town in Nunavut, meaning "where there are iglus."
igunaq	[ee-goo-nuck]	Fermented walrus meat.
Ijiraq	[ee-yee-rock]	Name.
Ikpiarjuk	[eek-pee-ark-joo-k]	A town in Nunavut, meaning "pocket."
Imiqqutailaq	[ee-mik-koo-tie-luck]	Name, meaning "Arctic tern."
inugarulliit	[ee-new-ga-rule-leet]	Mythical, mischievous tiny creatures resembling very small people. Generally the size of a rabbit.
Inukpak	[ee-nook-puck]	Name, meaning "giant."
inuksuk pl. inuksuit	[ee-nook-sook, pl. ee-nook-soo-eet]	Rock cairn used for aiding hunters and indicating direction.
Inuuja	[ee-new-ya]	Name, meaning "doll."
irniq	[ear-nick]	Son.
kamik pl. kamiik (2), pl. kamiit (2+)	[ka-mick, pl. ka-meek (2), ka-meet (2+)]	Boots made from sealskin or caribou skin, depending on the season.
katuk	[ka-took]	A drum beater.
Kinakuluugavit?	[key-na-koo-loo-ga-veet]	A phrase asking, "Who are you?" Often used in a diminutive way to someone the speaker finds cute or adorable.

Kiviuq	[key-vee-oak]	A legendary hunter, known in almost every Inuit sub-group.
Masik	[ma-seek]	Name.
Miki	[me-key]	Name, meaning "small one."
nanijauniaravit	[na-nee-yow-nee-ah-ra-vet]	"You'll be found."
nanuq	[na-nook]	Polar bear.
Natsivaq	[nut-see-vuck]	Name, meaning "large seal."
nukarlaaluk	[new-kak-laa-look]	An expression of annoyance at a younger sibling who is of the same gender as you.
Nuliajuk	[new-lee-a-yuk]	A sea goddess whose fingers transformed into all sea mammals. She needs to be appeased by shamans when she is angry.
Panipak	[pa-nee-puck]	Name.
Paninnguaq	[pa-ning-oo-ak]	Name.
Piturniq	[pit-oo-nick]	Name, meaning a time when the tides are strong usually during the new moon. Pitu for short.
puukuluk	[pooh-koo-look]	A term of endearment for the biological mother of an adopted child, translating to "beloved one who carried me."
qaggiq	[kag-geek]	A large iglu built for the celebration of the return of the sun. The word is also used to describe the celebration itself.
Qajaarjuaq	[kayak-jew-ak]	Name, meaning "large qajaq."

qajaq pl. qajait	[kayak, pl. ka-yite]	The Inuktitut word for "kayak." Traditionally made from driftwood, bones, or baleen covered in sealskin.
qallupilluq pl. qallupilluit	[kad-loo-pill-look, pl. kad-loo-pill-loo-eet]	A creature in Inuit myths that lured children playing alone on the ice in order to snatch them into its amautiit and kidnap them.
qarmaq pl. qarmaak (2), pl. qarmait (2+)	[kar-muck, pl. kar-maak (2), pl. kar-mate (2+)]	A house made of stones, moss for insulation, and whalebones used to hold up the roof.
qamutiik	[ka-moo-teek]	A sled made from many materials, such as frozen fish, moss, driftwood, and animal bones, which carries supplies and families, usually pulled by dogs. Modern qamutiit are made of wood and typically pulled by a snowmobile.
Qilak	[key-luck]	Name, meaning "heaven" or "inner peace."
qimmiq pl. qimmiit	[kim-mick, pl. kim-meet]	Dog.
qulliq	[kood-lick]	A lamp made of stone carved into a half circle, usually with moss along the edge and seal fat to keep the flame alight.
Saimaniq	[sigh-ma-nick]	Name, meaning "calm" or "happy." Saima for short.
sakku	[suck-koo]	A toggling harpoon head that separates from the spear and lodges into the blubber of the animal it hits. Typically it is attached to a rope that the hunter pulls to retrieve the animal.

Sikuliaq	[see-coo-lee-ak]	Name.
Tagaaq	[ta-gawk]	Name.
Taina	[tie-na]	Name.
Taktuq	[tak-took]	Name, meaning "fog."
Tiri	[tee-ree]	Name, but is short for "tiriganniaq," which means "fox."
Tunu	[too-noo]	Name, derived from the word for "back"
Tununiq	[too-noo-nick]	An area on Baffin Island around the community of Pond Inlet.
tuurngaq	[tour-ng-ak]	A spirit guide for shamans.
uakallangaak	[oo-ah-kal-la-ng-a-ak]	An expression of surprise, joy, annoyance, or confusion.
ulu	[oo-loo]	A crescent-shaped knife for women, with many uses from cutting meat, to skinning pelts, to cutting out patterns and more.
uujuq	[oo-yook]	Boiled meat.
Ujarasuk	[oo-ya-ra-sook]	Name.
Viivi	[vee-vee]	Name.

A note to readers: One sound in Inuktitut that might be more difficult for English speakers is the "ng" sound, which sounds like the "ng" in "sing."

Author's Note

This is a fictional story that was inspired by a lot of real people that I've met throughout my life. The characters were inspired by elders, teachers, leaders, a few people who were less than nice, and most of all, by my friends.

Many of the characters in this story were given the names of real people from my hometown of Igloolik. I chose to do this to represent the strength of Inuit naming customs. Inuit have passed on names for generations and I thought that using the names of people I knew was kind of cool.

This story is set in the old days before Inuit traditions began to change and adapt to include the things that whalers, traders, and missionaries taught Inuit. Though I tried to portray life in those days as accurately as possible, it's hard to get everything right, especially when there are many different versions of stories, traditions, and languages from region to region throughout Inuit Nunangat. The creatures, the magic, and the world are my own interpretation of the legends I grew up hearing, and I wanted to share that with Inuit youth more than with anyone else.

Growing up in the Arctic means you are growing up with stories that are thousands of years old. Whether it's mythological or true, these stories define our perspective on life, the universe, everything. Through storytelling, one gains confidence and wisdom. In Inuit culture, these two qualities ensure strength, endurance, and survival among our people. As we lose our elders, we lose a lifetime of wisdom. We lose unique stories of magic and we lose valuable rites that were practised for millennia. Young Inuit today are grasping to hang on to it, but time has a habit of being persistent, demanding, and forgetful. Through hard work and passion, one way of revitalizing our rich culture is having youth and elders work together to keep hold of traditional knowledge. We need youth to keep that knowledge as a part of who they are, and continue the tradition of sharing and teaching.

The great thing about stories is that they mean something different to different people. For one person a story could be an escape from reality, an imaginary land of good and evil, while for another it could represent the release of some very real emotions. So, I hope that those who read this story can gather their own meaning from it, and I hope that it is as meaningful to you as it is to me.

Qujannamiik,
Aviaq Johnston

Acknowledgements

The amount of people who have helped and supported me through this project is unbelievable. I would like to thank the Aboriginal Arts and Stories competition by Historica Canada for allowing Aboriginal youth to voice their thoughts and feelings in a creative and safe space. They have been instrumental in my success as a writer. I would also like to thank Neil Christopher, Kelly Ward, and the rest of the Inhabit Media crew who have given me the opportunity to publish my first novel.

I would like to thank the friends and community members from Igloolik, Pond Inlet, and Pangnirtung that recommended traditional Inuit names to me: C. Qamaniq, J. Merkosak, M. Mike, K. Merritt, P. Nutarariaq, K. Aqatsiaq, S. Ilgun, A. Arnatsiaq, S. Ryan, J. Stuart, J. Maurice, S. Quassa, and J. Kullualik. I am grateful to my coworkers Pauloosie, Parniga, and Imo for supporting me while I worked on this personal project between the obligations of my job.

I would like to thank everyone at Nunavut Sivuniksavut, specifically Morley, Maata, and Murray, for endlessly supporting me in my educational and personal success. Your advice has taken me to great heights and I am truly grateful to have your wisdom in my life. A huge thank you to all members of Artcirq for being able to tell amazing Inuit stories in a fun and entertaining way. Artcirq's 2014 show, _Asiu_, was one of my key inspirations for the story of Piturniq.

And finally, I would like to extend my thanks to my beautiful family and friends. I am unable to find all the words that can possibly convey how incredibly appreciative I am to have your love and encouragement every step of this long journey. Jackie, Todd, Ali, Marley, Aquack, and Terrie, thank you for being my biggest fans and always giving me praise. Stacey, thank you for always being super enthusiastic about my work.

I thank Kiah for always being so encouraging. Thanks to my cousins, Sianna and Arnaara, just because I love you. Jesse, Laura, and Niviaq, thank you for giving me a purpose for being the best person I can be. Thank you to my grandfathers, aunties, uncles, and cousins. I love you all.

Without my family, this book wouldn't have been possible. I thank my dad, Glen, for being excited for absolutely every aspect of this journey, from the first chapter to the editing process. I thank my mom, Elisapee, for being my cultural and Inuktitut guru. I thank my brother, Anguti, for being my biggest role model. I thank my sister, Alannah, for far too many reasons to write. I thank my nieces, Amy and Leah, for being the ones I will always try to impress.

To those no longer here on earth—Garth and my late grandmothers—thank you. I miss you.

And thank you to Inuit youth all over the country, you will never cease to motivate me to try my hardest to achieve great things.

Qujannamiik. Nakurmiik. Qoana. Matna. Qujanaq. Thank you.

About the Author

Aviaq Johnston is a young Inuk author from Igloolik, Nunavut. In 2014, she won first place in the Aboriginal Arts and Stories competition in the senior category for her short story "Tarnikuluk," which also earned her a Governor General's History Award. Her other works include "My Mother Tongue," published in *Northern Public Affairs* magazine, and "Language Revitalization," published in *Nipiit Magazine*. Aviaq is a graduate of the innovative post-secondary program for Inuit students, Nunavut Sivuniksavut, and went on to briefly study English at the University of Ottawa. Aviaq loves to travel and has lived in Australia and Vietnam. She spends most of her time reading, writing, studying, and procrastinating. She is currently living between Iqaluit, Nunavut, and North Bay, Ontario, as she completes a diploma in Social Service Work at Canadore College.